I0744653

Other books by Sherrie DeMorrow:

Knight and Daye
Cloud of Dreams
The Elder Rose
All The Land
The Little Bird
Beyond the Land
A Little Princess
Romancing the West
The Silver Millions

THE SILVER MILLIONS

BY

SHERRIE DEMORROW

Published 2019 by

Lightning Source (UK) Ltd
Chapter House,
Pitfield,
Kiln Farm,
Milton Keynes
MK11 3LW,
UK

Cover Art Design by Sam Wall

To LL for help and support

In acknowledgement of HS
and
To the memories of
JM, AC, JH, NW, MA, RS
and especially TO'C,
who inspired this story

PREFACE

Although this could not be mentioned before, please be advised that there are sections of this book, as in the previous books, that contain *actual* life experiences, emotions and memories. In the guise of fiction, it is the only way to inform the public of the results of an extreme lifestyle and treatment toward a helpless child (now fully grown and *still suffering daily, the aftershocks of such treatment*). It is to be further noted that this individual suffers from a spectrum disorder called Asperger's Syndrome, which is a form of Autism.   The author hopes this will not affect the enjoyment of the following, as well as the previous stories already written.

Despite the disclaimer in the aforementioned paragraph, please note this is still a book of fiction. The reader must suspend all preconceptions of belief in past history, as this book is not meant as an accurate representation of historical events (except in the case described in previous paragraph).

The historical attitudes towards sensitive issues, and people's prejudices of the time, had to remain intact to provide a sense of realism in the story. No historical figures represented herein had been harmed during the writing of this work.

Some place names given are **NOT** real, unless otherwise stated or recognised as real (or based on real places). Other characters (for the most part) are fictional and loosely based on people known of by the author.

PROLOGUE

Once upon a time in the year 2269 AD, there came about a scientist called Martin Augustus Chayten. Dr Chayten served the New England Foundation for Formulated Matter. He worked with dug-up theories and relics of the unsuspecting past, distant or recent. Most didn't accept his findings, as most of his colleagues there thought him too dangerous, due to his tampering with DNA samples found in the humane remains of the soil.

He was rivalled by many and reviled by just the same, with sneers of *'it will never work'* ringing inside his head, like a gong on television...

... then one day, he found an unusual DNA pattern within the formation of a tossed-aside rock, retrieved from a previous expedition near the southern edge of New Hampshire.

His examination of such distinctive matter would create the most devastating of consequences Man would ever know... either now...

... or in another time.

He huddled over his microscope all day. Flasks of liquid littered his desk (that were not fit for human consumption) and slaps of papered notes were strewn all about him like refuse. He tried desperately to make sense of his findings. He wanted to see the enlightenment of the comely extraction he was prepared to do...

... so his mind slithered and slid anew from typical formation.

He took an instrument to remove an oddly bit of a dust particle off the rock. With sterilised tweezers, he saw a slinky L-shaped entity and put it aside in a petrie dish...

... just laying around, awaiting the newcomer.

There were other bits of abnormal formations on this same rock, and, once removing them, he added them to the one already in that petrie dish.

Soon, the rock suddenly crumpled away, leaving no further tract of exhumation nor existence. It now became a pile of dust, leaving the scientist no choice but to add it to his collection...

... however, he DID remember to use another dish.

He took a pause from the intensity of his work when his secretary, Josephine, came in at that moment. She brought him a cup of coffee, which he gladly welcomed.

She asked him, 'Any luck on your testing yet?'

'Got some samples here. They look intact, as you can see,' Dr Chayten replied.

She peered through the microscope, then looked up. 'Yes, they do. Maybe you can create something from it.'

The scientist was most enthused at her comment, and surprised by her supportive nature. 'Yes, perhaps I can... to... to benefit Man, I suppose.'

'Playing God again?'

'No no no,' he droned, denying the idea (*the very idea!*). 'Just the usual tinkering to see what we could learn.'

'And what have we learned?'

'Don't fill up a petrie dish,' he smiled.

'I wish you the best,' Josephine walked out, 'Enjoy the coffee.'

She left Dr Chayten to his newest samplings...

... but what he didn't know was those new samplings began to develop and move around, as a cell does when offspring is created...

... the process of which cannot be reversed, for that would be murder...

... in some cases.

Dr Chayten examined the dish and gasped in wonder. Could it be a life form had evolved from mere samples taken from an overexposed rock on a beach, hidden in a slime-drenched cave? *The ol' girl was right, I was playing God.*

But he did not destroy the developing entity in the dish. He took it out in favour of a larger size one, so it had room to grow, to form an amazing mass of...

... of...

... Dr Chayten rushed to his allotted books to compare notes and findings. The notations were beyond his reach; he looked everywhere, as he realised this entity was unprecedented...

... and the finding was...

... peculiar.

The amassed formation turned into a ball, and paused its growth for the time being.

Dr Chayten decided to keep watch over this *being* and spent the night in his lab. It would prove worthwhile to see what this ball-thing would do next.

Night fell quietly, yet quickly, as the season ushered its autumnal equinox. Everyone in the Foundation called it a day...

... just as the emergence in the lab was beginning a new one.

While everyone was leaving, Dr Chayten was settling down in his small room, used as a contingency when his experimentation led him working late at night. In an adjoining room, there was space for a cot, a small dresser with a ready change of clothes and a small washroom/toilet facility. His all-nighters left him slumbering in the throes of his job he felt he needed to pull off...

... when most of his co-workers thought him an absolute fanatic in his dedication to science...

... but this night was to be an exception.

Within the DNA samples, atypical enhancements occurred within the materials selected. They bonded together and an embryonic *something* was born.

The night wore on...

... it seemed like forever...

... especially when that embryo had moved out of its dish...

... and into the dust of the larger dish.

Now, it lay silent.

Dr Chayten called it a night himself, tucking into his cot and turning off the light. He thought there was nothing he could do at the moment and his mind was already toxic with fatigue.

And so, he closed his eyes peaceably on the finality of the day...

... unaware of the finality that was to come.

CHAPTER I

It was a splendid sunny day for the latter part of 1691. The weather was calm and pleasing; not too much turbulence for me.

I served aboard the *Taylor Brent* under the command of Captain Christian Tempest Spey, an Anglo-Hispanic offshoot from the fabled Woodes-Hastings family. His great grandfather was Deveros, the eldest of the celebrated Spanish brother-explorers, the Del-Spays. Tales were told there was a meeting at Sydmouth Harbour, during the time of the Spanish Armada. Deveros had touched English soil (in more ways than one), and to prevent capture, he hid among the locals for a short spell...

... a spell for one young Woodes-Hastings maiden, who saw more action than the invading Armada itself...

... which awaited to strike.

When Deveros left port, he climbed aboard his ship to fight the English, and later died in the battle. Out of respect, she decided to allow further use of the Spanish surname to her offspring, but merely changed the spelling, (preventing awkward circumstances)...

... to become the Anglised *Spey*.

This seed of descent remained alive...

... it was a seed I now served under.

Spey was fair and true, but beneath his English exterior, lay a very impassioned, exotic and wild side to the fellow...

... just like me.

I was born Conna Timalyn Daye in Oconnalow, Ireland. My father was a seaman like myself called Elliah Daye and my mother, Nova Cayne, was a native Maltawah girl from Profesthermeth Island (so-named by someone with a lisp). I walked along a tightrope of racial divide, yet still sexy in my stride, as the half-gone-Maltawah portion of me dictated. The furry darkness of the body covered me, but the blue eyes stayed. I was adaptable, and never astray from the seasons.

When my father took Nova back to Ireland to take up the rites of Oconnalow, she was unused to the cold and damp nature of the land. It had taken its toll on her, as she obviously preferred her southerly Pacific environment. She easily succumbed to various colds, which turned into flu and fevers. She died suddenly with much mourning (but not unexpectedly), shortly after my birth...

... but it did not make her less of a person and we still honoured her with a good send-off.

And then it was just my father and me.

One day, he said, 'Find yourself a job in a ship's chandlery and get beyond the Irish Sea. Once you do, make a pilgrimage to Profesthermeth Island and meet the tribe leader Timbala, who is your uncle. You are part of your mother's tribe, and that must be honoured.'

I went out thus, and found a place that supplied the ships in the harbour. Years of hard labour set me off on my journey an apprentice, making candles, scraping barnacles off hulls and eventually, I expressed an interest to serve aboard. I worked on land before I got my first break, and soon served aboard a schooner, the *Peytannic*.

My life at sea began and I vowed to father that I would make the trip to the South Pacific. We were enlisted by the Admiralty to find a treasure hoard, known as the Silver Millions. *Silver Millions of what?* Apparently, word had spread about shimmering lights under the sea, as something metallic reflected from the shore's edge. Long ago, the Maltawah had the Millions hidden for centuries, until a rival tribe from Ohyto Island came along in a flash of frenzy and captured the booty. They were stopped by a European vessel and the coveted prize was tossed into the sea, depriving the newcomers a share therefrom...

... and the Natives thought to look for it later...

... but never did.

When the ship returned to colonise the island, it was wiped clean of the indigenous population. With all the carnage, there was no one left to look for the hoard. For the Maltawah, they didn't see any point to recover the treasure for themselves, because they felt it to be triflings of the civilised world. Although they may have been *influenced* by civilisation, they kept to their own, with an occasional visitor from here and there. After all, what would a fancy bauble serve in purpose to the unaided tribesman's eye? Maybe to present it to their leader? He *would have* gladly received it, but no. The Maltawah preferred a more simple warrior's life, to live for the hunt and stay fit for one another…

… in case of colonisation, remembering what happened to their rivals.

So, under strict orders we were to search for the Silver Millions, and claim the same for the Crown. Most, however, would rather claim it for themselves...

... especially one Spanish Captain Silvah Diaglo...

... accompanied by Spain, our ever-present bother.

Diaglo was a bit of a pirate, bit of a rogue, bit of a rake and a bit of what you would not wish to meet up with in a dark alley. A nemesis to Spey in more ways than one, this would not be the first time those two crossed swords together. He guided his galleon, the *Hola Rosaria* for those so-called Millions.

The *Taylor Brent*, too, sailed day and night, to commence the search for this ye-olde-clichéd treasure. I was a good hand at sea, as I worked hard for Captain Spey. I liked him and he returned the favour. I raced among the rigging, hoisting sails, along with other menial tasks. My favourite task was lookout duty atop the main mast. You could get a splendid view of the sea and any land that went with it, as well as privacy away from the other crewmembers (when personalities would heat up faster than a cannon).

The workday schedule was quite gruelling today. The sun baked us at half-mast, and we were half-clothed. Water was rationed to every seaman at Spey's command, and he saw to it that none shall thirst on his watch. The hours passed, and some men collapsed from exhaustion. I tried to be strong, so those around me wouldn't think I claimed the Throne of Wuss. I held out, as others just stuck on like a weakened tack.

Meanwhile, the Silver Millions sequestered beneath somewhere, too deep to do a thorough search. Its container rotted slowly in its hampered state, lid cracked slightly ajar...

... revealing a *glimpse* of the endless silver, ever-so wished for by Man...

... but naturally, the fish couldn't give a toss, though some were curious and decided to prise it fully open.

A newcomer came to join in. 'Hey, what's this?'

'Let's go and see,' another replied.

Fishtails suddenly beat at the helpless chest, aiming for the rusty lock, in attempt to release its permanent hold on the contents.

Another knock...

... getting closer.

They tried again...

... nearly there.

A passing shark wondered what all the fuss was about.

The fish duo trying it on with the object replied, 'We're trying to open this chest. Could you help?'

'I'll give it a go, but I'm not one to eat metal. Gives me indigestion.'

The shark leaned forward to catch the lock, which snapped open in a instant, with his large fang-like teeth. With the swoop of his tail, he blew the difficult chest wide open. The coins spilled out with the accompanying violent shake and scattered to cover the immediate area.

'There y'go. Your treasure is freed. Have it your way, m'lads.'

The shark swam away, now thinking of some *real* food.

The fish raced to look at the coins.

One of them remarked, 'Hey, aren't these the Silver Millions?'

'Course they are, stupid,' the other said, whacking his friend with a fin. 'How did you come to know about this, anyway?'

'Must be rumours under the sea.'

'This is useless to us fish. We don't care for metallic objects. All we want is a fine meal and sleep.'

The fish smirked, 'What about Matilda?'

'What do you mean? Who told you about Matilda?'

'I don't know, just heard about it. You skipped the lady-part.'

'Ya heard, ya heard. C'mon, let's go. This place could sure use some cleaning up around here. That's what dem dames are good for.'

'Why not ask Matilda?'

The fish continued to bicker over women and their impact on the environment. They both swam away, leaving the shining hoard behind.

'Someone will get it,' was their passing answer.

The sun above shone down on the sea and the Silver Millions were as real as the fish that swam around it. Nearly every ship in the area came a-looking, as the hoard silently waited for the lucky soul to capture it.

Since the chest was opened, the metallic coinage had shone clearly through the clear blue waters of the sea. Tropical storms eventually mislaid the coins, scattering them over the surrounding areas, and possibly much further. They swished around the bottom, catching out the fish, as they yelled *'Ow!'* when they got pelted.

CHAPTER II

Aboard the *Taylor Brent*, life continued peaceably, but for a few scuffles and resulting floggings. Spey was a fair man; not the old and tired type, but not young nor inexperienced. He was stationed within the middle ground, and embraced the nuances expected of someone at this time of life.

He watched the sea with intensive eyes; always through the spyglass, he searched for his pardon...

... and maybe a battle hum, resulting from the find below...

... *if* he was the lucky one.

He anticipated and savoured the moves of his opponent, Diaglo, though he silently conjectured how far he was in the search.

Those stationed at the lookout-on-the-main were most honoured to keep their post and, like me, they relished to get at the fresh height from the sea, with the exception of those who detested heights. From atop, you can see clear sparkling waters; never fading, never dim. Colonies of fish meandered in daily exercise, while other fish pursued them over an invitation for lunch.

Sunken vessels lay adrift on the sandbanks below the water line, where the Mercastes lived...

... *or so it was thought.*

You could see them in the transparent waters, if you knew where to look. Usually, it was their objective *not* to be seen. They were half-man, half-fish, and the species came in female varieties, too. Their origins were unknown, but it was guessed that they must have been around for some time, possibly from antiquity. *Who knew?*

Some sailors gave in to the females and drowned in their own stupidity, as the Mercaste would swim quickly away as soon as the Mortal hit the water. Mercastes liked to make homes out of the old hulks of sunken ships (the bigger, the better), and spent many a contemplative afternoon in them...

... but for now, my knotting skill was a contemplation on its own.

* * * * *

While Spey was in his cabin corresponding to the Admiralty, his second-in-command Robshaw, kept watch on deck. A lowly crewman called Jarris had spotted something underwater. It flickered with light, shining beguiling beams to beckon good chase. More bewitching than a woman's brew, it lay in a scattered heap, with piles of other shiny metal pieces stacked higher than others.

All and all, it was a tempting treat...

... at which point Jarris freaked out, screaming vivaciously around the deck. 'The Millions, the Millions. I saw the Silver Millions.'

'Now that's someone who'd been at sea too long,' remarked Cateliffe, with a gap-toothed smile.

'Aye,' agreed his counterpart Nay-Smith, 'And the Mercastes will show him their true nature.'

Both laughed among themselves, as they hoisted a newly repaired sail upward.

Robshaw stood motionless on deck, when Jarris deliriously bumped into him.

'The Millions,' Jarris cried out, continuing his rave.

Robshaw regained his balance. 'Millions, eh? Millions of what? Women awaiting your pleasure; them dancing in your head like a shoreline spectacle?!'

'Oh, please, Mr Robshaw, please. Trust me, I saw it with my own eyes...'

Robshaw cut him off. 'Then see an eye doctor. You just saw the sun glaring at you.'

'No, no,' Jarris begged him. 'Hoards and hoards of deliciously minted coins... oh, the gain... the gain... of it all.'

Cateliffe chimed in, mishearing the statement. 'Coins do not taste like mint. If you suck one, you'd get a leaden tongue.'

A nearby crewman, Dexx, shouted out, 'Don't forget to unwrap the foiled shells!'

Laughter roared faster than cannon shot during a siege. The noise got Captain Spey out of his cabin.

He stormed up on deck. 'What the devil is going on here?'

Jarris's flustered bellows now lacked air, yet he firmed up. 'Sir. I saw the Silver Millions with my own eyes. Loads and loads of coins down below.'

A riotous answer spewed from the men. 'Then go fetch them!'

Spey took Jarris away from the men. 'Now Mr Jarris, I want you to stop treating myself, Mr Robshaw and your fellow shipmates like clocks.'

'How am I doing that, sir?'

'You're winding us all up over the Silver Millions. Yes, we are in search of them, and if you wish, I can get someone to man the lookout and have a wee search through the glass. Would that satisfy you?'

'I bet you will find them, where I stated they were.'

'If they're there, I am sure we will find them,' Spey turned to the complement of crewmen. 'Now everyone, back to your duties. The excitement is over.'

Robshaw went to Spey's side. 'I'm sorry you were disturbed, Captain. It shan't happen again.'

'I should say not, Fir' mate Robshaw. There will be no floggings this time,' Spey teased, returning to his cabin.

Robshaw continued his watch, and took the helm of reason. 'Men, do not titter any further on Mr Jarris's account. Maybe he did see the Hoard. Maybe not. Maybe he drank too much...'

This time, Jarris cut Robshaw off. 'I did not, sir.'

He suddenly swung an air-raid about him; this was something you just had to avoid, or get caught up within, to be blasted high.

From my knotted bow, I watched the mock-festivity. I knew it was not festive, but the feast of emotional turmoil was too good to miss. However, I found myself feeling for poor Jarris.

He had an older resemblance that smacked of Admiralty, rather than of someone who would be caught up with the ranks of us impoverished. He had poise and dominance nestled behind those beady brown eyes of his...

... but eye doctor or not, if he saw a good thing, then I was one to cast my vote to his side...

... and oddly volunteered. 'I saw it too.'

Robshaw turned to face me. 'Did you?'

I thought to back down, knowing it was a fib...

... but I didn't...

... and knotted up a yarn instead. 'Yes, I saw it... a great mass of silver inside a fantastic hovel... so crammed in, the contents spilled out.'

'Yeah right,' Robshaw dismissed, mistrusting the wily Irishman that was me. 'Back to work everybody. Jarris, for your irrational disturbance, you stand watch this evening.'

'But Sir,' Jarris protested, 'I'm due for a card game with Cateliffe and Nay-Smith.'

'You can spend time with your mates later. Now, to your duties with you.'

Robshaw then walked away and talked amongst some standing officers aboard.

'Aye,' Jarris meekly surrendered.

The deck was cleared of the incident and everyone returned to their posts...

... except Jarris...

... who still felt *he* was right...

... and came up to me.

'I wanted to thank you for defending me in front of Mr Robshaw. Did you truly mean it, you know, in what you stated?'

I smiled. 'Nah, I just felt to stick up for you and pull the First Mate's leg. No one else did.'

'I won't forget it.'

Jarris walked away, leaving *me* in knots.

Then, out of the corner of my eye, a flash of light flickered on the surface. I put my rope down and took a closer look over the edge of the ship. There was a wide diaspora of coinage at the bottom of the sea, twinkling like stars around the swimming fish.

Shit, he was right! There was justification in his defence.

The other crewmen wandered my way to see where my eyes were going...

... and they saw it too!

Murmurings were floating upward like awoken ghosts, and they started to take Jarris's claim seriously.

CHAPTER III

The ocean at night was a calm, dark place. Long and wistful, always moving, though stillness was its favourite disguise. It took many a man with its ravishing beauty; it had a cooling effect, if one got too warm; it had a soothing effect, if one felt desolate...

... and one desolate man, Jarris, stood at his punishment post as the night wore on. It was rather crude of him to raise hopes up when there was none to be hoisted, like a bread recipe without yeast. He was unsmiling, nearly scowling; a silent dirge in the middle of the night.

Below sea level, there were mumblings going on of a different sort within. Not of fish, Mercastes or other things of oceanic origin, but something more distinct. It was the entity of the lab of the latter years that had grown considerably since its inception by the hapless scientist, Dr Chayten.

It was on that night when the creature grew and broke free from its limitations of its life in the lab. Dr Chayten went to sleep in the next room, unaware of what was happening to his charge...

... or what turned out to be one.

Being formed in the many dishes, it continued to grow, and release itself from its varied confines...

... until it was too late, and the creature decided to go for a stroll into the outer world.

The scientist Chayten had spawned a living, breathing monster about 179 feet tall. With all those feet, this monster walked away from the Foundation, bringing some of it with it, in chunks. There was nothing spared, not even Chayten himself...

... who forever slept in the rubble.

It walked unto the nearby roads, where vehicles of all-sorts whizzed by...

... trying to get past it...

... but it never stopped for them.

There were endless crashes, torn cablings, lights that didn't operate, and overhead vehicles that kept hitting against the creature's head...

... and the monster did not like that.

It took a swipe at air traffic that realised it needed to be stopped...

... but the monster stopped them first...

... then headed toward the pier, and into the sea...

... where it lay in hibernation, as its appearance was getting in the way of things.

The creature took a good look at itself, seeing that it was male. The name of the scientist, Chayten, had its appeal to him as well, so he adopted the name to be his own.

During his walk around the sea, the other fish wondered who or what he was... or was it a she? They felt unsure. They saw that he was more lizard than fish, and some of the much older fish thought him a possible throwback to the ancient dinosaurs their families once knew.

Suddenly, a shining, round piece of metal was spotted. Chayten bent over to pick it up with its three fingered hand.

It looked like an antique doubloon, when at that moment, a great chasm was formed and the bottom of the ocean fell out beneath him. He fell for some distance when soon enough, he landed with a loud thud that caused a massive ripple; a fissure in time and place. The water soon became pallid and its earlier dominance gave way to Chayten's arrival.

Though Chayten did not wish to cause harm, he couldn't help but wonder what happened to him, or where he was...

He swam up to the water's edge and peered out. He found himself in the middle of the ocean. He panicked and screamed aloud, *'Where's the pier? There's nothing but water! No broken buildings nor smashed vehicles or flying machines trying to stop me.'*

He then submerged and took a few fish in for dinner. He found the water did not taste the same as to where he was previously. *The fish didn't matter; they all tasted the same...*

... and water was water...

... but these waters, he realised, *were different.*

Continuing his walkabout, he hit upon a pile of coins, similar to the one he found earlier that transported him to *these* waters. The coins were still scattered about, left untouched by Man, yet toyed with by fish. Chayten thought nothing of these coins, but in a large heap, they looked significant. He overheard fish conversations mentioning the Silver Millions, but disregarded the idle gossip.

If behaviour came to him naturally, he reckoned these coins were lost or currently being sought after by one or many.

Yet another thing occurred to him...

When he looked on his body to find grey-silvery circular scaling all down his sides and back, Chayten laughed so hard, even the sharks were displaced.

'Hey, watch it,' cried one, 'Don't shake up the waters.'

'Yeah, get lost,' scolded another.

Chayten growled back at them, chasing the sharks away. He felt indifference to their complaining and found that he could play an improvised joke...

... for his body shone and was plated, just like the Silver Millions...

... which *he* could be mistaken for...

... *the pleasure of those who sought these coins, would get a load of me instead*, and Chayten laughed even harder.

Another fish swam up to him. 'If you want to live here, buster, you better get with it. Don't disturb where you're not wanted. Your presence here is like a tsunami. Sheesh!'

Chayten gave a final growl and snapped at the fish, swallowing it whole.

There, that did it.

He wondered if the fish were trying to tell him something or protect that treasure. He then made up a bed (or the like) for himself and decided to take a nap…

… while the coins just passed him by.

CHAPTER IV

The next morning, the skies were fair and blue...

... just an ordinary day...

... *I guess.*

As I did my routine tasks, I became engrossed in a reverie...

... an ideal...

... a woman.

I've been out to sea for some time, so I never paid heed upon the matter. I thought about this fervently, as I carried on mending the hemp-made rigging, and minding my sail. I desperately tried not to show a smile about my thoughts on female beauty. I feared that those around me would clamp me in irons, if I were to give the inner message away...

... *out of jealousy, perhaps??*

So I kept my dreams to myself, tinkering and whiling away the time with work, and wondering how I would get back to Profesthermeth Island, where my mother came from.

I couldn't last long on the ship. I was restless and bored, but willing to go with what nature brought upon me. Yet seeing the drudgery of people time and again...

... and again and again...

... could stifle morale.

Spey was pretty good to us, I admitted to myself. Robshaw was very eagerly an ambitious First Mate who had his coming. They were two very different personalities of men working together. Spey kept to himself, mainly. He did not like much interaction, and felt this separation would establish a hierarchy that could not be broken. His distance was his power, he felt, and the less said about it, the better. Robshaw was more *with it*, in regards to his handling of the crew. He stuck in there, as he watched us struggle on by, knowing that was where he was once...

... once upon another ship's time.

Though I pondered to think how he or Spey would react, if they encountered the Silver Millions…

... or even when?

My mind reverted back to the dream woman again. Thinking about a captain and crewmates was all fine and such...

... but bedfellows, they did not make...

... especially with me.

The woman I was thinking of had to be naturally good looking, strong, healthy, cultured to some level, maybe one from the Island itself, to take back to Oconnalow with me...

... where I could spread my shamrocks into ye,
'til your barren canvas of self was full of me.

I let out a quick laugh when Jarris told me to hush it.

Jarris... what a shipmate!

I could not imagine how *he* got on board, with his whining, crying cowardice, questioning orders, then trying to be above his station by policing others, and (himself) giving orders...

... he needed to board a vessel at his own station!

'Forgive me,' I blurted, returning to the mending.

'You could get us all in trouble for this you know,' he sneered, his brown, beady eyes glaring at me.

Well, excuse me for living!

I remained silent, because I know Jarris was the type to bait a trap and cause a scene...

... and so, where had I left off? *Ah, yes...*

... the woman.

I didn't care what she looked like, her colouring could be fair or dark...

... or be it a sexy native, for I was halfway there.

It didn't matter to me really what she was; all I wanted was someone to love, and for her to return it.

Ooh, the yearning, the burning...

... such a prize...

... lay, lay, lay...

I nearly swooned in the fantasy of it all, and fell over backwards. Jarris caught me.

'You dithering dope, Daye,' he chastised, 'You could get us...'

Robshaw came over, seeing a slight commotion, cutting Jarris off.

'Anything the matter?'

I stood to attention. 'No, sir. I've done the rigging. Is there another task I could assist with?'

Knowing the foray was heating up between Jarris and me, Robshaw assigned me elsewhere...

... atop the ship...

... and barked, 'And don't come back 'til tea-time. Understand?'

I gave a salute and climbed the flights of my accomplished handiwork, and went to the much coveted spot, taking over someone's shift. A seaman who served his time up there had come down as I went up, only to keep busy with my duties...

... duties which never ended...

... as the ship was constantly in need of attention...

... like all sailing ships.

I climbed and climbed and found that spot of rope with a lean-to post next to it. My feet were raw, callused, but thankfully not bleeding. I got used to the harsh feel of the rope early on, and expected not to have the most attractive spots of my own.

The horizon loomed ahead, as the sky started its highest-high. It was midday and unfortunately the most hottest. I did not care, for I had a small cap on anyway, and my skin was good and tanned, too. The Irish were quite fair, you know, but for the length of time in the sun, my tone adapted.

I perused the sea, the wavy mass of blue-white foam in constant motion, and I was in complete isolation from the rest...

... especially Jarris, who was quickly becoming a bore...

... and it was plain that the feeling was mutual.

I was most grateful I did not get seasick from the watch, as I cast my eye upon the vast ocean waves...

... *the deepest rapture I e'er did see.*

Suddenly, something... a light... flicked against the pattern. A light, with a metallic hue emerged, teasing the viewer to be...

... possibly...

... the Silver Millions.

Oooh, ooh, did I see that correctly?

I questioned myself, *should I tell? Maybe I should...*

... for if it really was the Millions, then I would be had for letting them go...

... and go elsewhere, only to be found...

... by the Spanish!

No, no... I served with the British, and I had to stay true to my duty to the *Taylor Brent...*

... so I called out, cupping my hands to my mouth, 'Silver Millions off the starboard bow!'

There, take that in your pipe and smoke it!

I watched carefully; those below scurried in hasty movements to the sides of the ship.

Jarris, in his ultimate self-righteous frenzy, shouted, 'The Silver Millions! I was right all along; *they do exist.*'

Spey overheard the vocal outburst and left the cosiness of his administration duties.

He demanded, eyes alight with fiery wonder. 'What's all the shouting for?'

Jarris screeched like a true howler. 'I was right. I was right, oh, to whom it'd been foretold, I said so myself... I was right!'

... and so, he raved onward.

'Robshaw, get me my glass,' Spey ordered. The object was handed over, glass to the eye, and he leaned over the side...

... but will the Silver Millions gaze back at him?

He spent a few minutes searching from the bow of the ship. He lowered the glass and turned to face us...

... and demanded, 'Who reported this measly find?'

Cateliffe was all too eager to volunteer. 'Daye, sir, he called out... said something about his Nutty Millions...'

Robshaw was impatient in his tone. 'Well, you'd better get this right, Cateliffe; anything to report is a good thing, but it needs to be accurate!'

'Yes, sir,' he saluted in return and walked off.

I was then called deck ward from below and climbed down the rigging, like the true primate that I was, and faced the all-too-mortal Captain.

'Do you realise what you did, Daye?'

I stood at attention, gulped, and remained silent. I had yearned to speak, as I knew what I saw.

'Begging your leave, Captain,' I began, 'There was a glimmer of coinage floating about below the water line.'

'I don't care if you saw the glimmer floating about on a clothes line,' Robshaw snapped at me, cruelly.

Spey held his hand out to his Second for him to calm down and shut-the-fuck-up.

'Now Daye... I had checked where you indicated about the coins. I had seen *something*, there was a wavering light, but we just don't have enough information to determine whether they were there or not.'

'Please sir,' I begged, nearly kneeling, 'The Silver Millions were there.'

'In what formation? Where they close together or split apart separately?'

'Ummm,' I had to think fast, lest I forget the vision I saw from atop. 'Close, I believe, to my knowledge.'

Robshaw shook his head in disbelief and thought naught of my report. Spey, thankfully had an idea...

... but it would be one I would later regret.

'Why don't we send a scouting party to search for the treasure underwater? We'll hold the members with a rope and they have free reign to do their own finding, to determine once and for all if the Silver Millions exist.'

Robshaw was still entrenched in disbelief. 'A scouting party?'

'Yes, a scouting party,' Spey confirmed.

The Second then agreed. 'It will allay further false alarms and quell the claiming.'

'Good. We'll have Jarris and Daye go under to seek the Millions,' Spey ordered.

Jarris and I both exclaimed, 'WHAT?!'

I carried on, 'Surely, you don't mean *us*.'

Spey went up to me. 'I most certainly DO... and that is final. One more claim, outburst, or feeling of certainty that you saw the treasure, will lead you to the brig. You do not understand what you are doing to this crew by giving vain hopes.'

I was crestfallen. *How could he think I would do that?* Jarris, most certainly, but *me?*

'I would never think to do that. I know what I saw and reported the same to you.'

'Good, and you will go and find the blasted silver and report its whereabouts to us, before you cause a war,' Spey ordered.

'You heard the Captain,' Robshaw growled. 'Get out of your uniform and rope up. You're going for a swim, you two.'

'The rope should hold you near to us,' Spey said, 'We do not want to lose good seamen like you and Jarris, now do we?'

Robshaw backed him, yet in mocking fashion, spoke, 'We'll keep watch over you both, so you can seek out this finely cut treasure.'

Jarris hesitated. I felt concerned for him and asked, 'You're not afraid, are you?'

He shuddered in place, stammering, 'It's...it's...it's that I cannot swim.'

How the hell did *he* end up in the Navy?

'You cannot swim,' I repeated.

'Aye,' he sobbed quietly, realising ambition overruled weakness.

The reckoning was out.

Spey and Robshaw looked at one another. Spey assured him, 'We will hold unto you, and you will not be freed from the rope. The slightest tug could be felt.'

'Oh very well,' Jarris surrendered to him.

'Serves you right for keeping to your story in seeing the treasure,' Robshaw roared.

Jarris knew better than to lash out at a superior officer. Had it been a fellow crewman, well...

... better left unsaid.

The ropes were secured to our now stripped bodies, and Jarris panicked all the way through.

'We're doomed, I'm finished. Oh God, God, do spare my life, if Thou willist.'

'Pipe down,' I cried, 'Do you want me to freak as well? Now shut it, and let's do this. We must be level-headed about it, if we are to survive.'

'Oh yeah? At what part of the level,' Jarris wondered.

What a smart ass!

Working with Jarris was a challenge at the best of times, but to go beneath with him, silently without breathing...

... now *that* was going to try one's patience, with only gestures to use to communicate.

The officers and crew saw us off, and wished us luck.

'We will be waiting for you. Give us the signal when you're ready to come up,' Spey replied.

'We will,' I smiled, and shook his hand.

'Good luck to ye,' he returned the smile.

'Let 'er go,' Robshaw ordered...

... and down we went, plunging into the fascination of the deep.

CHAPTER V

I returned to the surface quickly to take in some air and find Jarris.

'Over here,' he called.

'Great. Let's move.' I dunked myself back into the water and swam to accomplish our mission.

Jarris followed, as he hung on to me. I slapped his hand and told him to follow, not to hold on.

What a nervous soul he was!

Holding our breath for as long as we had to wasn't easy, and it wasn't long before scaredy-puss Jarris hovered above, to take in air. I tried to hold out, but soon even I had to run atop to breathe.

How the heck will we be able to find the Millions if we kept doing this?

I motioned to Jarris to go under and we stayed below to search for the Silver Millions.

Soon, the struggle returned, and my lungs needed air again; so did Jarris's...

... now that we started to search properly, the interruption would prove most inconvenient...

... and, as I was about to lose it, the water swirled around me and there was a Presence about in the ocean.

Nahhh, this couldn't be... this was unreal... insane...

... potentially mythological.

'Conna Timalyn Daye,' a Voice bellowed.

Damn, what's going on now? It could not be Spey. No one could hear this far down; I was out of earshot.

'Conna Daye,' the Voice repeated.

I could not speak.

'Do I have to intentionally drown you to get your attention?'

WHAT?!

Suddenly, a hollow space formed around me and Jarris and air was sped into our bodies. Once I'd found my voice, I exhaled violently; Jarris spat up excess water. It cause a minor scene, but he sorted himself out in the end.

I then asked, 'Did someone call out?'

'It wasn't me,' Jarris cried defensively.

'Who's there?'

The Entity goaded us. 'Who do you think, or are you mythologically challenged?'

'Mythologically challenged?' Jarris commented negatively, 'Sounds like an oddball to me.'

'Hush it,' I snapped back.

'Conna Daye, you have entered my Realm with your counterpart and spent too long here to survive. What do you have to say for yourself, Mortal?'

'I... I...,' I stammered, trying to figure out to whom I was speaking.

'We're on a mission,' Jarris confessed to the Voice, 'To... to find the Silver Millions.'

'Oh are you now?' the Voice cackled with laughter. 'You think you could get away with that haulage? Do you realise you are in Neptune's Realm?!'

I smirked, 'Let me guess, you must be Neptune.'

'OF COURSE I AM NEPTUNE!'

We shuddered, realising we *were* dealing with a god, but not necessarily one that someone would worship in this day and age...

... unless you were dealing with the sea...

... but as Christians, we tend to forget these things.

'You are Neptune? I thought you were mythological.'

Neptune spoke less harshly to us. 'The very Same, my child.'

Oh fu--

'I thought as much, you are challenged in some way. Just because Man no longer depends on mythology to explain his world, doesn't mean it no longer exists. You just choose to ignore us old gods.'

'We feel that we've outgrown the old myths and legends,' I said.

Neptune added, 'That won't help you survive underwater, will it?'

I realised the gravity of the position Jarris and I were in. Jarris remained silent the whole time; Neptune and I continued to converse together.

'So, you seek the Millions, eh? For yourself, no doubt,' the god scoffed.

'For my ship; for the Crown.'

'Who's Crown? I'm the only Ruler here.'

'For His Britannic Majesty,' I admitted.

'Oh 'tish, Britannic Majesty, indeed,' the scoffing continued, 'You lot seek treasure for all time to get lost in your pockets... for your Imperial gain, I suppose... and what is an Irish fellow doing, working for the British, after what they did to your people?'

'I volunteered, sir, as did my father before me. The British hold no contempt toward me, nor I them. I am a willing seaman.'

The Great god joked, 'Oh yeah? For whose womb?'

I blushed heavily, though that was most difficult underwater. Jarris was nearly beside himself with laughter at our conversation, but did not partake in it.

'I shall now enable you both to carry on your mission with a Kiss though in my opinion, you both should be drowned and returned to your blasted ship. But, personal pleasure and opinion aside, I will allow this only once.

'It is temporary. The effect should wear out in about, oh... an hour's time.
Then you're on your own and breathing will not be possible. Then I will
make sport of you... dig?'

I gave him a blank stare.

'UNDERSTAND??!'

The meaning was now quite clear.

'Much obliged,' I replied. I motioned to Jarris to move closer and we both
received the Kiss.

'You may feel a tingling sensation around your neck area, on one side. Pay
it no mind, it's your skin getting used to the gill I've just made for you.'

We put our hands to our necks and realised the change.

'Remember, you've got an hour. After that, may the Waves claim you.'

Jarris grovelled and kissed Neptune's hand. 'Thank you so much. Oh, you
gave us life again.'

'I'd give you a tailfin as well, but I'm guessing you're only here for a short
hop. I've helped your people over many years, Millennia even. You lot
are a proud race and at times, a pain in the backside!'

'We are proud. I guess those who lack understanding of ourselves would
think us a bore,' I replied.

'A bore is putting it lightly. Now go, before the waters close in on you,'
Neptune dismissed us.

We both were cast into the larger depths and swam around to get our bearings.

'God,' Jarris shouted, 'It's freezing!'

'Shut up,' I hollered back at him.

We carried on, and the ropes around our bodies remained intact. The ocean depths were now a breeze to go through, with our newfound power. If we'd held our breath *this* long, it would take a miracle to get us moving...

... and thankfully, the miracle of breath was more than what we'd expected.

The glimmering began to reveal itself again, just like it did above the waves...

... but this time, it was different.

I took Jarris by his rope and led him behind the Baska Reefs. We looked on in bewilderment, as we saw a huge pile of coins stacked up in a strange shape...

... but were these the coins emerging in a horizontal pile?

The formation we witnessed resembled that of a giant creature. What creature it was, was unknown and I thought my imagination was working overtime. I glanced at Jarris to see what he thought of this and he shrugged his shoulders and kept a short distance.

We swam closer to see what this was all about, hopefully not to be seen (if it was a creature), when…

... at bait's breath...

... an eye opened.

It had a golden yellowing colour, with a black slit for an iris...

... this was no flower...

... this was...

... this was...

I motioned quickly to Jarris to make haste and swim away, exceedingly fast. I tugged both ropes to inform the ship we'd concluded our journey...

... our mission...

... our defeat...

Neptune hadn't warned us there was a sea creature of that magnitude under the sea.

And when I silently enquired, He replied calmly, 'You didn't ask.'

I wanted to leave the formerly beautiful wetness behind me, and get back to mending that rigging...

... it would take much more to mend *my* sail.

The creature stirred and got up to look around to see what the commotion was. He said nothing and resumed his afternoon nap.

CHAPTER VI

I pushed Jarris and myself forward and onward, until we felt a lift to the surface.

We hurriedly raced our way to the *Taylor Brent*, where Spey, Robshaw and Cateliffe awaited us.

'You two must have been through quite an adventure down there,' Cateliffe remarked, removing the ropes from us.

'You were underwater nearly forty minutes,' Spey demanded, 'What happened to you?'

'Looks like you've been pulled through the wringer,' Robshaw added.

'The salt should heal their skins,' Spey said.

Jarris and I looked at each other and wondered where to start.

'It's like this, sir,' I began.

'No, Daye, wait, wait,' Jarris snatched the explanation from me, 'There's a terrible thing down there... a marauding monster, a bestial beast, ready to kill us all. Oh, the gain, the gain, what would have been the gain!'

Robshaw questioned, 'A monster?'

Jarris continued his rave. 'His back had the gleam and texture of multitudes of coins, but there are no coins and the treasure is nonexistent. It's a malingering behemoth!'

'I saw its eye, sir, it was yellow gold with a slit in the middle, like a snake,' I recounted.

Jarris hollered, 'There are no Millions, it's a monster!'

'So *that's* what you've been seeing all along,' Cateliffe guffawed and walked away.

Spey walked to another part of the deck. 'Legend has it that there is a monster in these fair oceans. We don't know what it is or where it'd come from, but all I know is that it's referred to as the Chayten monster. Chayten's a native word meaning *dreaded carnivore*. It's not much of a description, really, but unless you get up close and personal to it, it only marks it out as an identifier.'

Robshaw got anxious with worry. 'Can we defeat this... thing?'

'Defeat, unknown. We do not know the Chayten's purpose. It lives undersea and acts like all the other fish do... only he's of larger proportion and very distinctive from the rest. It's a wonder if anyone gets along with the Chayten.'

'Yet, his body proved a goodly deception,' I suggested. 'But if the Spanish are unaware...'

'You got it, Daye,' Spey shined on me, 'Do the Spanish know what lies beneath?'

Jarris smiled rather crookedly. 'So you don't intend to report this beastly bipedal?'

Spey laughed aloud. 'Certainly not. Lead the Spaniards into thinking there *is* a trove down there, and let nature take its course.'

'A war within a war,' Robshaw exclaimed, 'How complimentary.'

'No fighting, no weapon discharge, no blood; we win and rule the seas,' Spey's grin went further.

It sounded like a good idea at the time...

... until it was heard that the Spanish got wind of the Silver Millions being close within our section of sea.

* * * * * *

It wasn't long before the Spanish caught up with us in our quadrant. Captain Diaglo was quite intense with intention in his fury towards us.

'Sé que sabes dónde están los millones de plata. Los tienes; tráelos ahora,' he shouted.

None of us spoke or knew much Spanish... though we expected our beloved Captain Spey to converse with the fellow, as he was part-Spanish already...

... but *that* didn't mean anything, as he was later to prove.

'Go and find them yourself. The ocean's big enough for you. *Vamanos,*' he mocked, mostly in English...

... we knew what side he was on!

This ticked off our opponent, for his English was rather rusty at best. He tried it on anyway, as he didn't care what he spoke. He felt deeds spoke universally.

'*Tu vas, bastardo!*' Diaglo yelled forth, 'I bet you have the treasure. You know where it is. Surrender it to me, or we fire on your ship. '

'Do we now,' Robshaw challenged. 'Maybe we have it, maybe we don't.'

'No games to play with you, señors. You give or we fire on your matchbox ship.'

'What if we said there was a great sea monster down below whose back resembles the coins of the Silver Millions,' Robshaw heckled.

The answer was forthcoming. 'Oh yeah, and there is (*who is it you like*), a Santa Claus. *Mierdatoro*!'

And with that, the Spanish ship steered closer for a better aim...

... as a cannon shot out its ball, *heading for us*.

'Battle stations everybody,' Spey commanded, as we scrambled to load our guns.

Both ships fired on one another, doing damage to wood, flesh, and metal. Many panicked in the melee, but kept up in battle. Spey and Robshaw proved to us to be the good leaders they were.

Robshaw helped below decks alongside us.

'Make ready... fire,' he bellowed.

Up atop, Spey shouted his orders to fire.

Guns furiously pummelled into the *Hola Rosaria.* It was getting too close, when soon, some rascally-minded sailors of theirs boarded our ship (in an attempt to search for the Millions), taking prisoners from all sides...

... and I was one of them.

I tried to fight off my assailant, when he cleverly used a medicinal he stole from the medical supplies to knock me out. I was then taken to the Spanish ship and thrown into *their* brig below, locked up for good...

... or so they thought.

Our men and Captain were shocked at what transpired, as prisoners were captured and placed into cells on the other ship. Soon, I was with Jarris and Cateliffe. The other men fought like devils, and carried on fighting...

... no pulling punches...

... just flying into the faces of despair.

Some lost, some died. Those among us in the prison cells aboard the *Rosaria,* screamed and shouted colourful words against the Spanish. Their voices were soon silenced by the opponent's firearms...

… which proved it was better to keep your mouth shut.

Meanwhile, swords lashed out; sabres crossed violently on the *Taylor Brent.*

'*Los Millions, Los Millions,*' a Spaniard taunted.

'Not on your life,' Robshaw answered, with a few whacks and a thrust into the unkindly gentleman...

... and carried on as before...

Thrust.

Gash.

Lunge.

Draw.

Fight.

And so it was for a time...

Meanwhile, Jarris began to whine. 'What are we doing here? Oh, oh, we'll be a-gone soon. We'll never leave.'

The sobbing noises got to Cateliffe's patience. 'Oh, can it,' he barked.

I didn't contribute to the banter, nor lament at our situation. I was too busy looking for a way out...

... a means to escape.

I found the rotting wood around me was in a terrible state. I think some of it moved, or someone nestled an apartment block within...

... when I saw the fiery ball pierce the side of the ship's hull...

... and everyone knew what *that* meant.

'Get down,' I screamed.

We all crouched down, as the cannonball narrowly missed us, but hit another target...

... a wooden post...

... which smashed to pieces and woodpiles flung out around us...

... lucky we were still crouched.

The ball met its mark and a minor explosion took place. The ball's impact caused a fire to another wooden post...

... and we were very close to it and closed-in.

Jarris jumped out of his skin. 'How are we going to get out of here???!' He shook the bars on the door, but in vain, because they would not budge...

... which was the point of being put in the brig.

He started bawling heavily and Cateliffe and I began to formulate a plan...

... and took Jarris's laments to heart and screamed...

... 'GET US THE FUCK OUT OF THIS CAGE YOU DEMONIC WRETCHES!'

A Spaniard ran past and laughed at us. '*Adios amigos.* This too will pass... very soon,' he giggled as he raced above deck to a possible escape.

'You whoreson,' Jarris sniped, then panicked some more, 'What are we going to do... oh...!!!'

I noticed a small crack in the corner of the floorboard. A nail had become proud in its position...

... and I gazed at it longingly, wishing to God above I had a hammer.

Yet, as I did not have one, I had to use my hands...

... which I did.

'Daye, you idiotic imbecile,' Jarris spoke, 'What are you doing?'

'Trying to get us out of here, Jarris, which is better than your moping about and whining about it,' I shouted back at him.

Cateliffe grimaced at Jarris and lent me a hand.

'Thanks,' I smiled.

'Don't mention it,' he replied, 'To the Spanish.'

We giggled about, though we were hard at work, which was more than what could be said for Jarris. We wiggled the nail about to loosen it up, but the damn thing wouldn't budge. Cateliffe's hand started to bleed, as did mine...

... and the fire was getting close.

We carried on, like the trapped rats that we were, when the nail *finally* gave way. The pressure against us threw us back into a corner on the other side of the cell. I haphazardly bumped into poor Jarris.

'Merciless malignant,' he a-cussed me.

'Sorry,' I answered, 'but you did want the plank loose, eh? *You* want to be free of this place, right?'

Cateliffe went back to render the plank free from that unyielding nail. I ran to assist him and we yanked it to reveal the ocean...

... which was now gushing heavily *inside*.

'We must get off this ship,' I ordered, and took a few more planks away...

... making the once steady *Rosario* a sinking mess.

The fire had reached some powder kegs that stood beside the cannon.

'She's gonna blow,' Cateliffe yelled.

Jarris pushed him aside and plunged into the water. Cateliffe and I followed.

We all swam away into the deep, as fast as we could, far from the ship as humanly possible...

... when shortly thereafter...

... *BOOM!*

The explosion could have woken the dead, nearby fish, and maybe that Chayten monster, as bits of wood, human remains, and metallic pieces littered the once-calm sea. We were well away and under the blast, but I got separated from Jarris and Cateliffe. I went above water for a breath, and tried to locate them...

... no luck...

... and it would be the last time I ever saw them...

... for now.

* * * * * *

Meanwhile, Cateliffe and Jarris made it to the now-damaged, but intact, *Taylor Brent*. They hurried aboard, thankful in their misery to be among their crewmates. The Spaniards who boarded the *Taylor Brent*, had been killed off and cast overboard; the skirmish was thankfully over.

Robshaw met them. 'We heard what happened. Where's Daye?'

'Still in the water, last we knew,' Cateliffe huffed. 'The blast was deafening and immense. I honestly doubt he survived it.'

'I second that too,' Jarris agreed.

'But you did,' Robshaw snapped.

'Aye, that we did. Doesn't mean Daye did. We got separated and all we cared about was getting back to the ship,' Jarris snidely reported.

Spey came to them, relieved. 'Thank God, you've escaped.'

'Not Daye,' Robshaw murmured.

Spey felt helpless that he lost a valuable crew member... *any* one and *every* one was valuable to him. That was the nature of the sailing ship...

... and expected.

'Well let's take stock of the damage and what supplies we do have left, as well as the men. Get going,' Spey dismissed them.

Robshaw came up to Spey. 'Will you be holding a service for Daye, sir?'

Spey turned to him. 'We shall, though we do not know the design of his fate; he could be *out there* somewhere, dead or alive. What we do know is certain, he is no longer with us. We must remember him for that, at least. Ready Reverend Squeamish for service.'

'Aye, Captain,' Robshaw stated, saluted, and went to find the churchman.

CHAPTER VII

I swam the sea again, taking in air as I could, then plummeting down to carry on my survival. A familiar rush occurred and the Voice began to roar out my name in a full gulp.

'Conna Daye, you have returned. What have you come for this time?'

I spun around to face Neptune again. 'Yes. I'm here once more.'

'We can't keep meeting each other like this. I must give you the Kiss.'

'Ah well,' I scoffed, 'If you must.'

A protective shell around my being allowed me to breathe in. It was not the usual ocean fare, but it was like a Presence inside a hollow cave. I felt gills forming on my neck and suddenly...

... whoa baby, I've got a fish's tail!!!

The clothes ripped off around me and I was naked under the sea, but for this weird appendage I now had to get used to.

'Dear Conna, as you are here again, and I am uncertain as to your duration, I have transformed you into a Mercaste. You can live and breathe down here to your comfort, and you might as well look the part. Now, what the heck brings you here?'

I gasped in amazement as I wiggled my lower half, swishing it around to get used to it. I was perplexed at the mythology even more so, as I had no thought to actually *becoming* a mythic being!

Neptune noted my tail-about. 'Do you like your newfound status?'

'It makes it easier to swim down here, yes,' I smiled back.

I carried on practicing twirling about, and adjusting to this *power* I had.

'Now, enough of your fooling about, Daye! Again, what are you doing here,' the Great god demanded.

I explained my ass away this time. 'We engaged with the Spanish; some of our crew were taken prisoner by them (myself included), and put aboard their ship in the brig. A cannonball landed below decks and shattered the wood and posts around us. There were barrels of powder which exploded from the fire made by the cannon shot. Then, the Spanish ship blew up.'

Neptune listened intently. 'So you had no other purpose being on someone else's ship.'

'We were forced aboard. We were prisoners.'

'Where are the rest?'

'Mostly dead. The two men with me, Jarris and Cateliffe, got separated. We escaped into the water, before the ship exploded. I do not know their fate and I hopefully assume they'd made it back to the *Taylor Brent*.'

'Your ship?'

'Yes.'

'They have.'

I murmured a quick thank you...

... it had not gone unnoticed. 'Don't mention it.'

'The Spanish boarded our ship after attacking us, in a hasty bid for the Silver Millions or its whereabouts. We told them about the sea creature.'

'Chayten,' Neptune confirmed.

'Those blasted fools didn't believe us, and continued their intended argument to ill-purpose; a fight to the death. Who knows where my ship is now?'

'Going back to England,' Neptune presumed, 'And they declared you lost... not dead, yet not alive either. They're planning a honorary service for you.'

'Not a funeral, then?'

'Art thou deceased?'

I drew in another breath... *duh!*

'Well then, duh back to you,' Neptune teased.

'That blast was pretty intense,' I added.

'I bet it was. Hard to believe your friends made it back to tell the tale.'

I floated around and looked at mine. 'Guess they won't be able to tell this one.'

'No, they would not. Listen,' Neptune offered, 'Care to meet the Chayten?'

'You want *me* to meet the Chayten? Yeah right!'

'Well, it will be a fantastic opportunity for you to see it close-up and to confirm your beliefs regarding those Silver Millions.'

'Our mission previously had failed,' I said.

'I know, cos you were frightened by the monster. He ain't bad, once you get to know him.'

I gulped... *get to know him? What does this Fellow take me for?*

I uttered nervously, 'Surely you're joking.'

'I am not. No joke at all. Come on, he's a nice fella. You will see once and for all that the treasure is really the creature himself. The actual coins everyone keeps yapping about are well scattered away, into the fathoms below. Well out of reach, and without proper human equipment, no one will find them without dying.'

I felt twenty years embarrassed, but I sucked in another breath and felt a kindly vibe from the Great god.

He beckoned, 'Come, I will lead you to him.'

Like I need friends now? I stretched my arms out and swam alongside the Presence of Neptune. It took some doing to find the lazy beast...

... and soon enough, we found him.

Neptune and I hovered from a distance. 'Well, here he is,' Neptune stated. 'Isn't he a beauty?'

'Maybe to another sea monster,' I joked.

He gently cussed me. 'Posh on you!' Then, the god called out, 'Chayten dear boy, come and meet the Mercaste Daye.'

The sleepy creature grunted and heaved himself up, granting us permission for us to draw near...

... wow, was he a massive one!

His whole body was covered in grey-coloured, disc-shaped scales that resembled the silver coins the crew and I were after...

... as well as everyone else on the high seas!

The display was a treasure in itself to see...

... but never to take.

The monster now sat up. 'Is this the one?'

'Yes,' Neptune introduced us. 'This is Conna Timalyn Daye. Conna, this is Chayten.'

'Hi. My Captain told me all about you. He claimed you are a legend.'

Chayten went all bashful. 'A legend, me? A fright, maybe, but I'm no legend and no portrait painting either.'

'Your surface is very attractive to us,' I replied.

'Yes,' Chayten looked himself over. 'I do resemble what you humans call the Silver Millions.'

'Was that *you* we kept seeing? I knew I saw something in the waters that day.'

'Yeah, you saw me a-nappin'. I sleep a lot these days. Nothing to do. I apologise for the ruse, but when I saw coins laying about, my footsteps seem to propel them elsewhere. Sorry about that. I thought I could play a joke. No one seemed to accept me down here, except maybe Neptune. After all, I was grown in a laboratory, many years...'

The creature stopped talking. Neptune signalled me over. 'This is the tricky bit,' He said. 'Chayten here doesn't understand he's been transported back in time. That is why he's so different...'

'... and so glittery,' I guessed.

'Yes. Of course he would not comprehend *reversed passage*, nor its consequences, for he is only a dumb animal. It's his power of speech that freaks all the fish out. The growls he made more recently had scared many schools away. These sounds mimic your English language, for some reason.'

'If he is from the future, that could explain it,' I conjectured. 'Maybe this lab-place he referred to earlier might have had something to do with the language bit.'

Neptune's smile nearly broadened the sea. 'Or maybe I taught him, just for a laugh.'

I stared blankly, 'You...'

'Ah, ah... remember who I am now,' Neptune warned. 'This fellow might need a friend. You seem to need one too.'

Compared to Jarris, Chayten would be a piece of cake!

'Are you thinking of going back to your ship?'

At this rate? 'No,' I answered. 'They must be far by now, and you said earlier that they declared me lost at sea. I don't have much family. Just my dad, and I have no idea if he's alive anymore.'

'You'd been away too long,' Neptune bemoaned. 'I'm sorry. You're on your own.'

I looked at the Chayten monster, then at Neptune. 'I need to go to Profesthermeth Island. My mother is from there and I must meet what's left of her family.'

'You can bring your new friend with you to the land of the Maltawah, the tribe of the island. Scary beast good advantage in native relations,' Neptune giggled.

'You expect me to bring a sea monster to a primitive island? You've got to be off your rocker, matey,' I shook my head in disbelief.

'Awh, but look at him, Conna Daye... look at him. He needs a good cuddle and a walk, mind you.'

I turned to the creature, his eyes widened in child-like anticipation. He didn't come across as a loser like Jarris, nor as smart-mouthed as Cateliffe. He definitely was not debonair like Spey, nor did he possess hard-nosed ambition like Robshaw.

'Fine,' I reached out to Chayten, as if he were a lost puppy. 'I'll take him.'

'Good for you, Daye. Good for you. Now, my boy, be warned…'

The catch was revealed…

'… you will lose your tail and underwater breathing ability, when you reach the Island. I trust you will want to stay there. If you re-enter my Realm, you will do so as a Mortal and take a fresh breath of air like every other Mortal does. It is my courtesy to you,' Neptune stated.

'I accept this. I enjoy swimming and, in future, shall do so as a Mortal', I consented, 'But let me enjoy the tail, please.'

'You may for a spell.'

'I shall remember to hold my breath,' I promised.

'Good, for if you do not, you will die. Now off you go!'

Neptune left us, then Chayten and I swam the journey toward Profesthermeth Island.

CHAPTER VIII

It took nearly a week for us to find the Island. The fish were most helpful in leading the way for us. My tail swished hard, as if upon a summer skillet. Chayten just did his usual walkabout...

... only for a longer time...

... and with accompanying *thuds* reverberating through the sea.

We fed on smaller fish or fish that proved an encumbrance to our journey. I tried to talk to Chayten, so treating him like a fellow. This proved a challenge, as beasts normally were more interested in partners, food or sleep. It was fun to only listen to the grunts emitted after speaking to him. It sounded like a word, and it took some time to really understand this guy, or *creature*.

We worked our way to our destination when Chayten growled, 'You never found your Silver Millions, did you?'

'Nope, though you made up for it. My fellow crewmates went nuts upon seeing your body's reflection in the ocean,' I answered. 'You made a good mirage, and just as deceptive.'

'Thank you,' he grinned.

'We planned to use you as a joke against the Spanish.'

'I planned to use me as a joke upon everyone.'

That figures!

'When we get to the Island, will you remain in the ocean, or live on the land, with me? It would be hardly a warm welcome for you, if on land.'

The creature stared at me and sighed. 'How do you humans put it, that *beauty is in the eye to behold*?'

I smirked in return. 'Good enough... whatever.'

'I think it best for me to stay underwater, out of the way. I have heard tales and recollections from other fish about monsters like me who venture out to the human world and make chaos of it. That happened to me when I left the lab all those years...'

I coughed and spat out, 'Yes, yes. That should be fine. You shall stay underwater.'

'There are plenty of schools down here anyway. I could enrol in one,' Chayten thought aloud.

'Probably to mind your manners,' I reckoned.

We trailed off; soon, I came upon some Mercastes hovering about.

'Your Island is nigh... some odd miles away. We wanted you to know,' one of them said, pointing the way, then quickly swimming out of sight...

... before I got to say thank you.

I raced to the top of the water to take in fresh air and see where the heck we were. Chayten held me up and I had a good glimpse of the surroundings. We were right in the middle of the great sea. I looked around and found a shoreline far off in the distance, with foliage covering the land.

This must be it, though I did not expect to see signs such as *Welcome to Profesthermeth Island. Please hold your course steady*, and so on.

The monster lifted himself above the water's edge. 'See anything?'

My height increased, but my balance tipped and I fell in...

... and the resulting splash had startled Chayten. 'Sorry,' he said. 'I'll try again.'

'No, no. I'm fine.' I struggled to regain my bearings. It was just like being on a ship, though in this case, I *was* the ship!

I headed for the land mass I spotted, with Chayten following at a close distance, this time underwater...

... for he could only keep his head above water for only so long, and that was not due to breathing skills...

... this dude was ugly...

... and probably would freak out any (or all) Islanders off the map!

I felt a tug at my tail end and went under.

It was Chayten. 'You know, I think you should go on ahead now. I will stay here, at a safe distance... we don't want to scare anyone, do we?'

'No, I guess not,' I concurred. 'You don't really look bad to me.'

'It takes time to know someone. I did not know my master, or creator. I think he had died during my escape from the...' the creature lamented.

I felt sorry for him, but cut him short. 'At least I got to know you.'

'Guess you're on your own now, Conna.'

'Yes, I guess I am.'

'If you do need me, I'll be here.'

'I will no longer have underwater abilities,' I said.

'Neptune will help you again, if you need it,' Chayten affirmed. 'As for me, there are plenty of things to see in these waters. How would you put it... *I shall have a field day.*'

'Alright, Chayten. I will miss you and it was good to travel with you.'

'Same here. Just remember, your tail will disintegrate upon land. You may need to find your footing again.'

Like I needed to be mothered by a sea monster!

'Thank you, and I hope to see you again.'

'I look forward to it. One of the few humans, perhaps only human who ever offered me friendship,' the monster stated.

''Tis the best ship to board,' I smiled and bade farewell.

I swam alone this time, unhindered by fish, large crazy talking sea creatures like Chayten, or even Neptune Himself. Everyone knew I was swimming toward the Island, and after a few further strokes hence...

... I hit the final run to the shoreline...

... whereupon, I had retransformed into a normal human. My legs and feet emerged and I spat out a lot of sea water, deeply exhaling. My lungs cleansed themselves with fresh salty sea air. I felt like a downed vessel that just flopped on the beach. I was tired, hungry, slightly cold...

... and naked.

I tried to stand to get something to cover myself up with...

... FLOP!

I fell into the sand, feeling a fool that I was. There were plenty of trees about...

... determined, I tried again.

One step, two step...

... whoops!

Shit! I couldn't get upright.

I felt quite helpless and frustrated. The agony of not being as mobile was annoying, and I'd wondered if this happened to other Mercastes, if caught out on the land...

... maybe it takes a bit of time for the strength to return.

I saw someone staring at me through thick green leaves. I dared not call out, for fear it could be an enemy, or worse...

... but then, I had made friends with a sea monster!

Nothing should stop me now...

The thick green leaves moved...

... the rattle became louder...

... the thrashing of a wind that was this person...

... or a thing?

The torment teased in my mind, and I could not do a blessed thing about it...

... I tried praying...

... Our Father, who art...

'Hey, I say ol' man, are ye hurt?'

I felt an inner jolt. *It speaks English!*

'Hey,' I called back, waving.

The figure of something, which I thought was some *thing*, emerged as a young woman.

Ohh, this was pleasant... how nice!

She asked again, 'Are ye hurt?'

'I'm not hurt, but for pride,' I answered her.

'Pride? What are you on? You're just laying around.'

I felt embarrassed at what I was about to tell her. 'I swam for a long distance, determined to find Profesthermeth Island. I was turned into a Mercaste to allow myself the luxury of the distance, so as to not drown.'

Giggling, she figured it out. 'So Neptune helped you?'

I was shocked at her *stab-in-the-dark* answer. 'Yes he did, as a matter of fact. I served on a British ship. We had an entanglement with the Spanish over a treasure known as the Silver Millions. It turns out the treasure is really a behemoth called Chayten. It was said a few coins were tossed about, free in the ocean, but this Chayten fellow has scaling that resembles the coins that make up the Silver Millions.'

'So that's what we saw at sea, before we were wrecked,' she recalled in awe. 'What's this Chayten like?'

'I thought you'd be keen on Neptune.'

'Nah, Neptune is a myth. Chayten, at least, showed himself.'

'How do you know it's a 'he'?'

She grinned. 'How do you don't?'

I pouted. She made good fencing style conversation and I was beginning to like her.

She was not a Maltawah, but a white girl with fair skin. Her hair was dark honey coloured, and long. Her eyes pierced with brown earthen meaning. Her clothes, though, reflected that of the Native culture on the island.

She saw how I looked at her, which did not go unnoticed. 'I've been here for some time. My family and I were headed for the colonies, when a storm hit, or maybe that Chayten friend of yours, and we washed up ashore here. Most of the passengers, including my grandparents, had died...'

Her countenance changed.

'You've survived,' I observed.

'The way you just looked at me, wouldn't *you* allow me to live?'

I took back my remark, as the eternal intonation reverberated in my head...

... *duh!*

I stuck out my hand. 'I'm Conna Timalyn Daye.'

'I'm called Cindihan. The Maltawah here couldn't pronounce, or care about what my original name was, so they renamed me Cindihan, for a legendary figure our Leader knew about.'

As did I. 'Cindy, then,' I agreed, when I noticed I was still naked. 'Um... could you get me a little something to cover myself up with?'

Cindihan got spooked with realisation. 'Ooops, sorry. We were talking and you still lay there. There is only so much sand, you know. I'll find something.'

She ran to the hedges where she took some vines and larger fig leaves for me. I attached them to my body, as best as I could, to make modest of an awkward situation.

'You shan't get a rash, it's just temporary, 'til I find ye some decent rags,' she said.

She went away and I looked around. The surrounding greenery had flowers and plants of various colours. Fruits grew way up high and you'd have to be a real animal to climb up to get at them. *Maybe the Maltawah were good climbers...*

And still, I waited for a bit longer, hopefully not too long. A guy could catch a chill by the shoreline.

I turned away toward the ocean and thought about the *Taylor Brent*. I'd wondered if it made it back to England, how they treated my departure, and, of course, how Jarris was doing...

... when soon enough...

... a call burst through those trees. 'Conna, dear Conna!'

I spun to face Cindihan. She held a long piece of hemp fabric and gave it to me. Naturally, I bundled myself up within it; *ah, that's better.*

She said to me, 'Chief Timbala will see you now.'

CHAPTER IX

'Timbala?' I mused over in my mind, aloud. 'You mean Timbala Cayne, brother of Nova Cayne?'

'Yes, Conna,' she answered. 'He's the Leader of the tribe.'

'So he is... you know, he's my uncle,' I blushed proudly.

'So you're that fabled son of Nova Cayne.'

I smiled at her. 'Sure am. Let's go and meet him, shall we?'

I gathered up the loose ends of the fabric and tucked them into pockets of fabric that overlay upon me. Then, I was led by Cindy to the great Chief Timbala.

We walked inland and a clearing was ahead of us. A multitude of huts had been built close within, as if it were a city. It made for a nice snugly atmosphere, if you got along well with your neighbour...

... however, if conflict started, well, I hardly would care to think.

Within the larger section of the hut complex (if I may call it so), stood a makeshift throne made of bamboo, and various wood pieces with ornate carvings of symbols and animals. Strings of ivy had surrounded the entity, which made it more decorative. A pale skinned man in his mid-fifties sat there, adorned with a wide, multicoloured necklace that hung over his bare and hairy chest, reaching his shoulders; a feathery headdress resembling that of the Native Americans (which varied in style) with small horns pointing upwards; and his bottom portion was surrounded by decorative tree bark.

He certainly looked exotic enough... but I sensed something else about him.

His hair had a fine silver edge to it, as the formerly brown wavy locks gave way to grey waves. If he were about twenty years younger, he would have been a challenge for all the women in his tribe.

At most, he was extremely attractive and available...

... though many women went vicious to compete over him, but none of them survived the Ordeal…

… and so, he remained single…

(… *yet, this didn't mean he couldn't have fun on his own terms.*)

The Ordeal was the Maltawah's version of competitive sport, culminating in the election of a new Leader. Growing up in Oconnalow, with tales of the legendary King Muffyhuer and Queen Lowry Cindihan, I had no clue about the Ordeal; nor were the hidden secrets of exotic culture, such as that of Profesthermeth Island, revealed.

I was taken to the bamboo throne, where Timbala was sat.

'Greetings,' Timbala said, motioning me to come forward. 'You do not need to kneel, as you are my kinsman.' He looked at Cindy. 'However, you, Cindihan, must.'

He had her bow to him, and she happily complied.

'Hello,' I called out, extending my hand.

The Chief accepted and we shook hands. 'You are most welcome. I trust this is a social visit?' Then, Timbala spoke to the girl. 'Cindihan, rise.'

'I was told to make the pilgrimage to meet with my other half of family, to which you belong,' I announced.

'Splendid. We must catch up,' Timbala said, eager to listen.

'I sailed with the Royal Navy for some time; recently, there was a treasure hunt for what was called the Silver Millions, but it turned out to be a sea monster with shiny, metallic-like scaling...'

Timbala interrupted, 'This sea creature... would it be the Chayten?'

'The very same, Chief,' I confirmed.

'Oh, dispense with the formality. You are my nephew. Anyway, what else?'

The man was eager, wasn't he?

I carried on the tale. 'My ship fell into conflict with a Spanish vessel called the *Hola Rosaria*, led by a Captain Diaglo. He thought we knew where the treasure was, or that we actually had it with us. His men boarded our ship, the *Taylor Brent*, and took prisoners, of which I was one. When we told him it was the sea creature, he didn't believe us, and the prisoners were sent to the brig on the other ship.'

'The *Hola Rosaria*?'

'Yes.'

Cindihan listened with glee. 'You've certainly been around, haven't you, Conna?'

I grinned back at her, 'Do let me finish. Anyway. There was a fire aboard the Spanish ship. I, along with two other prisoners, tried to escape through the rusty-nailed, worn down floorboards. When the fire reached a critical point, we freed the floorboards and dived into the water. We swam far enough away from the blast, and I assumed the other two I was with, made it back to the *Taylor Brent*.'

Timbala asked, 'So what happened to you?'

'I'm here, ain't I?' I chuckled, 'I swam and swam, then it was getting difficult for me, keeping my body fresh with air. No normal human could survive that long in a deep stretch of sea. It was then I was assisted by Neptune, who transformed me into a Mercaste.'

Cindihan and Timbala looked at one another in astonishment. 'A Mercaste?'

'A general term used for describing mythological creatures of half-human, half-fish. I turned into one; then later, I met the sea monster.'

Cindihan cried, 'And lived through *that*? Get out of here!'

'Your phrasing is unnecessary, o'mischievous one,' Timbala chastised, then said to me. 'Do go on.'

I giggled at some point, seeing the ridiculousness of my experiences, however true they were. 'Neptune introduced us, and together (Chayten and I) we swam to Profesthermeth Island.'

'And that's when I saw you, Conna, tripping over yourself,' Cindy chimed in. 'You seemed such the spectacle.'

'Yes, but not the type you read with,' I joked. 'Cindy and I met on the beach. She thought I was hurt, so she helped me.'

'Oh, how charming,' Timbala cooed. 'You must stay with us; you are family, and now that you've been acquainted with Cindihan...'

She blurted out, 'There may be competition.'

I was puzzled. 'Competition?'

'Never mind, dear Cindihan,' the Chief dismissed, explaining. 'Silly button cannot keep her trap shut among guests. You know how girls are.'

I stared at Cindy and gave her a hug. 'Yes, I do.'

'My story is not as elaborate as yours, Conna,' she pouted.

'Well, I do not think you would have gotten one better than mine.'

'It is a relief to be here. I really do not like sea travel, especially cooped up with grandparents and others foaming at the bit to get to the Americas. I do not see what is so great about it. I like it here better,' she said.

Timbala agreed. 'It is more pleasant here. And we did away with those undesirables, didn't we?'

She smiled.

I glanced at the Chief in horror. 'You don't mean...?'

'Ah, you got me there,' Timbala sighed. 'How do you mean for us to live?

'The girl's grandparents were a nuisance aboard, I was told; widely disrespected among the ship's crew, and even in their Germanic homeland. They treated Cindihan terribly, and the gods only know how she was treated back home.' He looked up. 'Ah, it was lucky they actually headed in the wrong direction. You see, the whole crew and manifest of people were useless. Only Cindihan, who *we* renamed, has been worthy of my people... and, of me.'

He let out a savage shriek, to which the other Maltawah joined in.

I held Cindy close. 'I trust you do not wish to unload your burden, now. You seem intelligent and charming. You are very pretty, too.'

'You are lovely, Conna,' she professed, 'But no, I would rather move on. Maybe some other time, when the winds calm down in my soul.'

'So beautifully put,' Timbala stated. 'However, she is not yours... yet.'

I turned sharp. 'What?'

'The Ordeal, nephew. It determines skill, humility, endurance and determination of our warrior race. No harm will come upon you, unless you are too ambitious, and disobey the rules of fairness and nicety.'

Christ, what have I gotten myself into this time?

'You shall dine with us on wild boar, berries and wine, with a few leaves mixed in.' Timbala called his second, Ansarah. 'Prepare the feast to honour our guest.'

Then he ordered Cindihan to look after me, as the food was hunted down and prepared, as he so willed.

CHAPTER X

After dinner, I found myself in the company of Cindihan, and Chief Timbala Cayne. I had wondered how long the two of them were on the island, or if they indulged in a relationship of some kind. It bugged me the way he looked at her, *as if to care... possibly further.* Yet, as I never had a woman before in a proper manner, my eye was cast upon Cindihan...

... for it was I who truly craved for her.

I recalled my daydreams of the fair sex aboard the *Taylor Brent.* The passion of such an entity gave way to self-doubt and insecure feelings. I wondered if I was man enough to handle one. I could handle a ship, but a woman...

... that was yet to be seen.

Timbala started the conversation, after a good gulp of wine. 'So Conna, how long had you been at sea?'

'Most of my adult life,' I admitted. 'I etched out a small living on the harbour doing chandlery work, when I joined up on the *Peytannic.* My life had begun then, and my father told me I had to go to the South Sea islands to meet up with my mother's family, notably yourself. So I am here.'

'You joined the Royal Navy, I suppose?'

'Yes.'

'Was it what you expected, or would you like it better as a settled-down land master?'

'Eh, it had its moments; it has its rewards.'

'I heard the Silver Millions are still at large,' Timbala stated cautiously.

Cindihan drew a breath and took in her drink of fruity wine. 'Treasure hunters?'

My gaze came upon her. 'You could say that. It's either we find it, or Spain does. We don't want the Spanish to gain more funding from the ocean for their exploratory projects. They would prove the Royal Navy rather wanting, and our reputation cannot allow for this. Eventually, they will find more colonies to send their people to and settle down in. We can watch their leadership fall and rise and fall again into the latter ages, like a hyperactive sun.'

I concluded my theory about the Spanish colonial temperament when Timbala asked, 'Any more wine, Conna? Your cup could use a filling.'

I handed my cup to him and he refilled it. I took a sip. 'Thank you.'

He smiled back. 'I like serving my people. It teaches humility that most leaders enjoy to forget.'

'Sounds like you've been exposed to Christian teaching,' I observed.

'We have come into contact with some people, such as explorers, pirates, and settlers, who think they could survive island life here. Some of their culture and beliefs had rubbed off on us; we're not all that savage, you know. Not in the way some people think. Now take Cindihan, for example...'

All eyes went on her. She cried defensively, 'What?!'

Timbala addressed her, 'Those fellows and family you'd travelled with. They were of an older and inadaptable belief system. The Old Ways, yes?'

Cindihan showed a side to her that even I could not comprehend. *She must have been through a lot.* 'They were crap, they were false claimers and they coerced me into it! My mother's family took over and controlled my life, since she died and my father was forced to give me up to *them. It was such an unnatural existence to live in such an inane, archaic lifestyle. I did not choose this!!*'

She began to cry, brewing with such resentment and bitterness, it made me question myself in regards to handling a woman...

... especially a woman of so much tender delicacy.

'Hey hey, easy now,' I tried to soothe her and gave her a hug.

'This is what we had to work through,' Timbala lamented, 'She was in a really reviled state of mind when we found her. We had to wring it anew with love, patience and discussion. Naturally, we had the occasional disagreement that heated into a raving argument.'

I turned to Cindy. 'You argued with Chief Timbala?'

'I did,' she confessed. 'Timbala was kind enough to hear me out and work with me through the pain and anguish my maternal grandparents had caused me. After my natural parents were gone, they adopted me from an early age to prevent my real father from having me as *his* child. They took away any opportunity for me to see him for myself. They also used religion as an excuse to exert abuse upon my mind, while keeping up their fraudulent act.

'My mother's family came from Germany, and they were Catholic for many generations previous. But a few generations or so ago, an ill-gotten union was so desired, and the two in question decided to run away and elope... preferably elsewhere. As they were on the run, they could not get married in a church, due to parochial laws. There was a place they could marry in, but it was a place that upheld the Old Way. They paid whatever, and got married, as if they *were* of the Old Way. There was no formal initiation on their part: *they snuck in, falsified their identity and carried on, whatever.*'

I was stricken with grief when I heard this...

... as she continued. 'Their attitudes were insufferable. To be stuck travelling with people like that, was too much to bear. Thankfully the crew was too stupid and too drunk to hold themselves up, and they spilled the beans. I found this out from one of the crew who noticed the intolerant behaviour my grandparents had showed me. He wanted to tell me everything, and did so, under the cover of night. On a small ship, space means all, but the space could take all, too. Yet, I was so privy to much dirt, my hatred for them and their disgraceful religion had grown to obvious proportions. The ship was rigged to fail and eventually, we ran aground, as I stated earlier.'

'In that storm,' I confirmed.

'Or the Chayten, but there *was* an intention on the crewman's part, in order to save me from this horrible deceitful family. The beaching was a Godsend.'

I asked, 'So, what about your father?'

'He was Italian. That's what I was told on the ship, cos I never met him. It went even further that his family dates back to ancient Rome, and an ancestor had been part of the Legion that had gone on the subsequent invasion forces to Britain. Not early on, but maybe a hundred or so years later. I think there could be a link-up somewhere, because a great part of me pines to be there. I was told of a possible Celtic connection.'

I smiled, thinking of a scheme to get her for myself and away from Timbala... *no offence to the Chief.* 'Would Ireland do?'

'Oh yes, please,' she begged. 'Will ye save me?'

'Cindihan, Cindihan,' Timbala coaxed, 'You needn't beg. You've already been saved.   I've given you comfort here, and taken a shine to you.'

There, he admitted it.

She met him, wide-eyed. 'But you're the High Chief of the Maltawah! I'm just this boring plain-song, it-thingy. Who the hell would want *me*?'

Now it was my turn. 'How dare you say such nonsense, when this great Chieftain had looked after you since your time on the island?   I am ashamed of you, selling yourself short.'

'I have nothing to sell and I *am* short,' she retorted back.

I sighed, when Timbala came to me and whispered. 'It can be part of the Ordeal to fight for this lass. Though she does not believe or know it, she's a genuine treasure, vastly worth more than the mere Silver Millions.'

I agreed and shook his hand. 'Settled. I'll fight for her any day.'

'Now nephew, Conna Timalyn Daye, I have a confession to make.'

I waited patiently. *What the heck would a Chief of an indigenous tribe need to confess to?*

'My real name is Silas Timothy Hathaway,' he said.

* * * * * *

Well, that was an earful. This certainly explained the curiosity.

Timbala continued his share of family history. 'I am not only related to you by marriage, through my adopted sister and your mother, Nova, but my connection to you goes back further.'

I stared at him in disbelief. 'You're saying we are blood-kin?'

He answered me. 'Yes. In the late 1500s, oh, I think it was the 1590s, there was a seaman called Elias Daye from Oconnalow, Ireland. He served on one of the exploring ships of Queen Elizabeth. He was on shore leave in England, when he came across a beautiful girl called Jane Hathaway. Like all sailors, he had his way with her one night and the next day, he left for the sea; fate unknown. This union gave way to a boy, and she took it upon herself to raise him under the surname of Hathaway. He later served for the Crown, as did his son afterward. Then it came down to myself, and I was led to the vast oceans of the world. A hefty storm blew things out of proportion, and my ship went down. I swam toward the nearest island, which was this one, and the Maltawah took me in. I was cared for by a tribesman called Cayne, who raised me as his own, as an addition to an already large family.

'Although I was very young at the time, I soon learnt the ways of the Maltawah and got tried and tested through the Ordeal. Inevitably, I came through flying and became the new Chief, when the previous one passed on. There was much competition for the empty throne, and as warriors, we tested our men, to see who was worthy of the garland to fill the space. *He who secured the seat first and released the ladder of opponents, won the Leadership.*'

Timbala paused, catching his breath. We caught ours, too, as we thought about Cindihan's story being equally tumultuous, yet just as worthy.

'We are blood, then,' I shook his hand.

'In more ways than one,' he answered smiling.

Despite a reconciliatory air around us, Cindihan burst out, 'But the attitudes of evil!'

'No,' Timbala chastised. 'The evil, as you knew it, has passed. You saw what we did to your grandparents and the others on that ship. There is no evil here; don't bring it 'round again. The Old Ways are dead and gone. *You are made anew...*'

... and with that, he took Cindihan and carried her to the shore. He walked into the water until he was waist-deep into it. With an intended throw, he cast her in and gave her a good splashing that could not be forgotten easily.

When she surfaced, the Chief came close to her. 'As Leader of the Maltawah and as a Christian (for I do subscribe to those beliefs), I baptise thee Cindihan, in the name of the Most Glorious Trinity, along with the Host of the Deities of the Maltawah…

'... arise your soul, my sweet, and consider yourself part of a Higher Calling and a Higher Being; and furthermore, do shut the fuck up about what you had been through, because cowardice and pining is not allowed in *our* community.'

I sniggered, unable to keep in the laughter.

Timbala turned to me. 'Wish to be next, Conna Daye?'

I stood to attention, as if in the Royal Navy again. 'No sir. I had the pleasure of baptism at Oconnalow.'

'I'm sure you had,' he cooed endearingly. 'You will undergo the Ordeal and participate in its every move. I cannot wait to witness your performance.'

He walked away, still in a joyful lull. Cindihan exited the water, drenched and exhausted.

She asked, 'What's he laughing at?'

'Don't know,' I replied, 'But I have a feeling we'll be in for it.'

CHAPTER XI

'In for what?' asked a quizzical Cindihan.

I stared at her. 'How would I know? I'm just as much a stranger to this island as you are.'

I wandered about, seeing many Maltawah with long flowing emotions, having their way with Nature, either through hunting or battling away to themselves to keep fit and able at a moment's notice...

... so they say.

I looked around me, as I walked through corridors of palm trees with Cindihan, hand in hand...

... and I thought I was falling in love with her, as my intentions escalated toward a finality...

... which was something to take up with Timbala...

... or Silas Timothy Hathaway, to you and me.

I reached out to her with my whole being of my blood and chased the skies around her. I was no longer bound to the Royal Navy's iron-clad lords of whim. I felt free, with them thinking I was deceased or lost at sea. There was much to be said for this. Timbala needn't worry about dear Cindy. My thoughts intermixed between caring for the young lady, and a yen for a natural feathered conquest.

'I want to go snowballing down a mountain with you,' I cried aloud to her.

'You may shout your deeds with me, but it is up to Timbala,' she answered in return.

I took her over to the side of a tree. 'Look, what is it with you and Timbala? Tell me honestly. Do you have a relationship with him?'

She hesitated and skipped back into her thoughts. 'He did take care of me, as he was cared for by Cayne. After the Maltawah destroyed the ship's compliment, I learned from the Chief and participated in tribal routines.'

'So, he kept you on.'

'I guess it was the story of the other crewmen that made up his mind about me, and to have me spared. He saw me as a hard-luck-case and all that.'

'And all what?'

She remained silent and walked toward two silent figures of the earth. 'That could be us.'

I walked up to her and examined the statues. 'Could be, but they must be gods of some kind.'

'Could be consummated lovers,' she guessed in a trance.

'You and Timbala?'

'Me and you?'

I sighed. 'Perhaps.' I put my arm around her.

She giggled and held me close. 'I doubt that. They were here long before my arrival, maybe even Timbala's.'

'Or even before mine, but we needn't split hairs about it.'

We embraced and began to kiss heartily.

A warrior approached us.

'You've got the Spirit of the Wakka-Wakka that slowly feeds and exits to bring you good fortune,' he said.

He walked away.

We giggled when he was out of earshot.

I was bemused. 'Wakka-Wakka? Sounds like an olden-tyme game.'

Cindihan chimed in with, 'You eat pellets and chase the ghosts away. What a drive!'

I glanced at the statue of the two again. 'Maybe there's something to all this Native tribal belief.'

'What, chasing away the ghosts of the past?'

'Maybe,' I stared in awe.

'Your string is showing,' she observed.

I checked my tunic. 'Don't allow me to reveal all my explosives at once.'

I fell into a daydream, similar to that I had on the *Taylor Brent*, but this time, it was more concise...

We felt like animals about to mate. Her soul, though, embodied a horrible malevolence brought on by her grandparents. Yet, like anything, a hot-temper could be defused by a cool wind...

... and that wind was me.

With a look of bedevilment in th'eye,
A wave of excitement ripped through my mind.
A full wind blew into my Celtic knottery,
When I flew dragon bat-shit to the moon.
And, with bated breath,
I could not see beyond her coverlet.

Then she cried out, 'I love it when a man comes together!'

I spilled my excitement away, as I confessed, 'You drive me crazy, but you're a good driver.'

She took away the elegance of my dexterity.
I drove to be inside her liberty, keen.
I believed I had saved her from the cruel deformity of spirit,
Once upon a knight brigade.

My mind went a-flutter when suddenly a voice yelled out, 'Ah go soak your head in a bucket of spit!'

I panicked. 'Cindihan?'

'That wasn't me. That's the Maltawah in the forest.'

'Must be testing upon each other in combat or such,' I supposed.

'They're as thick as excellence, don't you think?'

'Like a bipedal dot in the open countryside,' I laughed.

As the earth fell away, I said fuck you to the stars...

... in not so many words...

... for I truly loved Cindihan...

... and it was duly noticed.

'I don't mean to go against the snowflakes, but you must do battle to win me,' she said.

'I'll just take a good wow in a cave with ye and take th'air with it,' I answered back.

'Conna, the Chief doesn't have airs about him. He *is* the air.'

'Such splendid indifference makes fools of us all.'

'The movement is freaking me out,' she cried in awe, 'Timbala's an angel tipped in heavenly majesty.'

I gave her a look of concern. 'He's just a shipwrecked so-and-so from England, and got lucky, that's all. There's nothing special about him.'

Now she gave me a look.

I then growled, 'Or is there?'

'No,' she defended, 'He is that special because he'd won out in the Ordeal, in the part of the tournament that decides upon a new Leader. He told me of his experience and how he managed to out-do many Native adversaries.'

'Is that due to his English ingenuity or just brash-chic bravado?'

I loved a good fight and I could not wait to knock Hathaway off his pedestal...

... *Chieftain, my ass.*

She read my mind. 'You'll never make it.'

'You think not, eh?' I huffed, quite loudly, 'Well, look at this!'

I showed her my pecs, which I gained through my time in the Navy.

'I think you'll do nicely and could easily challenge Timbala,' she said. 'We're always in the search for new blood around here.'

'What about those from that ship you were on?'

'They were penny-wasters, very cheap and abjective. That's why they were put down.'

'I see... and you weren't?'

'Timbala saw something in me that sparked a light in him. He felt I was different from them, and knew I could get past the troubles they caused me.'

My envy rode a horse of its favourite colour. 'So he made you his flame?'

'I told you before, he just looked after me. I don't see any reason beyond that. He thought I was better than them,' Cindihan said.

I gave her another look... *the look o'the obvious.*

'Alright, fine. Maybe he was a tinge attracted to me.'

Ah-ha, she finally admitted to it, at last!

The hackles rose even further.

'So you like him? He's pretty olden.'

'Of course I like him! He filled in the gaping holes left by those nefarious grandparents since the wreck.'

'Sounds like there were more gaping holes to fill...'

She snapped, 'Now what is that supposed to mean? He came along and took me in.'

'Where?'

'Anywhere!'

'Had you ever...?'

There was a pause so thick, a sword could slice it in half.

She hesitated... again.

I continued to press. 'Well?'

She looked at me, still silent.

'And??!!'

This was getting annoying.

'Yes,' she admitted, 'But not in the fullest sense. He didn't want to hurt me and preferred to have me saved, either for himself or someone most worthy.'

I stood up. 'I can be that person.'

'I believe you can.'

'Yet, I shall not entrap you. If you desire the Chieftain more...'

'That's why we have the Ordeal,' she interrupted. 'We fight for what we want and win it fairly. The prize is ours to take, once it is won and finalised.'

The day was the longest I'd ever encountered. A hush fell over the side of the mountain and birds twittered along their cable-branchèd networks. The sun was past its prime edge and nearly ready to go to sleep.

In the distance, yet close enough to see, Timbala was walking along a path. He glimmered past us like a small torch; *the salvation and salivation of a young girl's mind.* He was burning bright, half-clad in golden brown velvet, with silver lining around the elbow and knee joints, and midriff; his exposed upper chest swimming with greying hair. His cape of delicate braid whipped in the transparent wind. I nodded to acknowledge his presence, to which he accepted and returned the favour. He went by us, towards his hut, where he would change for the evening's pleasantries.

I then asked, exasperated, 'Do you want him or me?'

'I confess, Conna, you're more earthly and practical. Timbala's a fable-come-true. Unreachable, yet, always there, with longing.'

'Cindy, I do understand,' I smiled, anticipating his eventual defeat...

... not to think of it as disrespect, you know...

... for it was the way of things...

... *the way of the Maltawah.*

Evening came and our minds departed for better things. Meats and fruits were brought out in front of the dais where Timbala sat. We were seated at the table in front of him, among the other Maltawah.

Timbala spoke, 'Be silent. Be silent. Bow your heads to the gods, and give them thanks for what we are to receive has been most plentiful.'

A guttural acknowledgment emerged among the others, as everyone helped themselves to the food.

Timbala then addressed me, 'Conna, tomorrow you will train for your participation in the Ordeal.'

I sounded *shocked*. 'Me?'

'Yes, you, Conna. You will train with Ansarah. You will make a fine warrior, and a potential for Cindihan,' the Chief commanded.

'Well, well,' Ansarah smiled, 'This should be most challenging.'

I shyly grinned, 'Now, I don't want to put you through anything...'

'No, no trouble at all.' Timbala soothed my concern. 'It's the way of things here.'

'Yeah, so they say. You know, for an Englishman, you're pretty up on Native culture.'

He took a sip from his cup. 'For a Maltawah-Irishman, you fit the bill.'

The other tribesmen giggled, as anticipatory tension filled the air as quickly as the many incense sticks beside us.

I asked Timbala, 'Will I *fight* for Cindihan?'

He gave me a stoic look and intoned soberly, 'You will fight for *supremacy*.'

The feasting went on for over an hour, along with traditional singing and dancing. The Maltawah were a friendly, hospitable group, but it would be intriguing to see how these qualities fare up against vicious competition.

CHAPTER XII

While I went off for training with Ansarah, Timbala had met up with Cindihan in his hut.

The hut was rudimentary at best, but as he was the appointed leader through victory, his hut was more lavishly decorated. There were sacred symbols, both native Maltawah and Christian, the latter coming from previous visits of European ships, his own included. Colourful native tapestries lined otherwise bland greenery of boredom. A double bed lay in a corner, next to a makeshift dresser. It would have been occupied by a partner, or even a wife, if he had one...

... but they all lost and died during the Ordeal.

Women braved their hearts and minds upon one another, clawing themselves silly into a catfight, over the most wanted and desired man of all the Islands...

... *Timbala.*

All had fought, all had lost to one another...

... and in defeat, their pride dictated a ceremonial killing of themselves...

... despite the fact that hara-kiri was not the most popular dish on the island. In recent years, the practise had been discontinued, and it was up to skill and ingenuity to see one victorious.

Though back then, to kill for the love of a leader was a most sacred honour...

... to murder or maim, for the one you truly love...

... the competition was fierce, as death became them.

Cindihan knew about these stories, from living amongst these islanders. Savage and strange, these island stories burned beneath them...

... and Timbala was no exception.

He had to brave it out, and to know once and for all, her loyalty.

'Cindihan,' he said, 'You've spent much time with Conna Daye of late.'

'I was getting him comfortable for island life. I reckoned he'd need a bit of companionship and know-how,' she answered.

'My dear girl, what I'm about to say is tendering my loins a bit, so I must be sure of...'

He paused.

'Be sure of what?'

He looked upward at one of those sacred symbols on the palmed wall of his hut.

A quick breath of prayer was said...

... then he faced her. 'Do you prefer Conna Daye or me?'

'I cannot answer that,' she dismissed him, walking to the bed and sat down.

'You know I am not an exotic like the other Maltawah,' Timbala sighed.

'Conna told me you were just a crafty Englishman who got lucky. You are nothing special.'

The Chieftain was amazed at her response, and exclaimed, 'He said *that*, did he! Well now, the game has gotten much more tempting and juicer.'

The lust for triumph shone behind his Caucasian blue eyes. You could smell the bodily pheromones in the air. The Native ways caught up to Timbala, as he let out a shriek of impending victory...

... or so he hoped.

As no one really could tell at this time who would win,
Though the stakes just got higher;
And he could not wait to fight his opponent
By the briar.

'Conna was in the Navy, you know,' Cindihan intoned, despite the hasty and dashing bravado displayed before her.

'As was I, ol' girl, as was I,' came the calmer reply.

'He looks very fit, and could well win against you.'

'He could... try,' the glint of passion remained, as Timbala stared at her. 'But...'

He moved closer and joined her on the bed, putting his arm around her.

'... but what?'

Timbala whispered, 'He will fail.'

'That's up to Fate to decide,' she surmised.

'Or the gods, or God, or whatever.'

He smiled, as his heart beat faster and his wish upon her never wavered.

'I told you in the past when you first arrived, that I would never hurt you.'

She remembered, 'You did, yes.'

Yet, how long would this last....

... the tension was extremely high...

... and soon he came closer to her...

... and kissed.

The exquisite ardour took them both by surprise. They drew near (and tighter), like heathen cords 'round one another.

'I still won't hurt or compromise you,' he promised, 'There is another way out.'

With that, they fumbled beneath the waves, which were becoming hectic and demanding indeed.

'You won't tell if I don't,' he panted, rubbing her.

'If Conna asks me again, I may have to. We discussed this before.'

The action halted abruptly and Timbala panicked. 'You didn't...!'

'I just told him that you wouldn't hurt me, and there was *something*.'

'That's more like it. Discretion of valour must be secured.'

'I wish to secure you, Timbala.'

His eyes widened wildly. 'Really?'

'If you win the competition, of course,' she added.

'Gee, thanks,' he droned sarcastically. 'But let us continue...'

'We must.'

That feeling arose within her and she felt better, sighing with relief.

Timbala needed to be sure. 'Got it?'

'Yep. Your turn.'

She went to his lower regions and pleased the Chief to no end, until...

... the shouting could not be controlled within the hut.

A warrior barged in, as Timbala grabbed a blanket to cover himself with.

'What do you want?' Timbala demanded.

'Anything the matter, my liege?'

'No, thank you.'

'It's the Wakka-Wakka, I can see it in the room,' the warrior teased. 'The smell of it ripens the air.'

Cindihan's face revealed a questioning look. Timbala cleared his throat and pointed at the door. 'And will you kindly close the door on your way out.'

The warrior left at that point. He then sighed, 'Cindihan, where were we up to?'

'No good, I believe,' she giggled, 'I thought you've caught up to that.'

With a twinkle in his eye, he mused, 'One could never catch up with love.'

'Or that sea monster.'

Timbala froze for a moment, forgetting their earlier conversation. 'Sea monster?'

'The Chayten. Conna told us about him, yeah?'

Chayten, Timbala repeated to himself. 'Funny name for a creature.'

'I believe that beast was responsible for the shipwreck,' Cindihan commented.

'You told me it was the drunken, ignorant crew that did your ship in,' he argued.

'Anything's possible,' she said, 'But I thought the drunken, ignorant crew story was more credible, which it was, cos it happened. There was a minor surge during that point anyway.'

He stopped to think. 'Yeah, maybe... that creature could have risen from his nap and set his sights upon the world. How much do you know of Chayten?'

'Only that he's responsible for the legend of the Silver Millions that everyone keeps on about.'

'Yes, yes. Actually, there were coins originally. Then, this thing emerged, and with it, the wildcat stories-of-the-sea.

She looked at him unabashedly. 'I cannot wait to see you in the trials.'

Timbala moved closer to her. 'I cannot wait to defeat your Conna, my sweet; you know I will.'

'You may lose to him, or call it a draw.'

'Whatever,' he replied softly.

The hunger was longing; a sweetest kiss pursued them to the lips, as they pressed upon one another once more. They breathed heavily and outwardly, as Cindihan's shortened fingers lightly touched Timbala's skin, making their way toward the lovely hairy hedge on his chest...

... lightly tickling the soft flesh of the sides...

... caressing the shoulders and neckline...

... with an intentional plunge downward...

... followed by a screech of insanity.

Timbala quickly interrupted. 'He flies, you know.'

She came up from her manual dexterities. 'Flies?'

'The Chayten has wings, or a turbo booster pack,' he teased.

'Yeah right, in your side,' Cindihan furiously tickled the dear Chief...

... who further screamed with excited glory.

They then laughed and gave each other a hug.

They paused.

She asked suddenly, 'So that's it? You're a devil of a tease.'

'Only until it is official, and you have fairly won me,' he winked at her, 'I was most sensuous, wasn't I?'

DUH! Was he ever...

'It's nice to know you care about me, not to infringe upon my person,' Cindihan spoke, clawing desperately to control her whim.

'I am the leader,' Timbala boasted, 'I must care.'

'Though this holding back is driving me crazy,' she admitted.

The Chief smiled at her, continuing to embrace and fumble about. 'It is the test of a true warrior.'

* * * * * *

In the meantime, my training was going along well. Being in the Navy, I had plenty of practise when it came to physical fitness...

... after all, the job itself was *based* on physical fitness...

... or you could not do the job at all!

I was secure in the knowledge I was good enough to face the Ordeal, even with a faint possibility of winning...

... either Cindihan or supremacy...

... Timbala could have the latter; I'll take the girl, please.

Ansarah had been a good trainer for me, and a fair opponent, too. He was thirty-five or so years old, well-toned and muscular. He was very attractive, with his dark, swarthy looks, a small moustache and short cropped hair. I was certain he'd be island-bait for the women.

God, if I could see them now...

... fighting in spit and glory...

... for him...

... for Timbala...

... the match would be most satisfactory.

We spurred and sparred one another with wooden poles.

'That's it, up more, Conna,' Ansarah instructed.

I deflected the attack with my pole and kept on volleying. Blow by blow, I swirled around to match his every move...

... and I think I did it!

Then, we pursued hand-to-hand combat. We moved in a peculiar fashion, eyeing greedily at one another, in order to take the other out...

... finding the way in...

... finding the weakness...

... and *blam!*

I lunged at him, as he tried to come after me. He then picked me up and threw me in a nearby pond.

'Hey,' I called out.

'Get used to it. We will be doing this over water.'

I was rather surprised and intrigued. *Water sports?* Unusual for a change, but then again, the Maltawah were an island-based, warrior race.

CHAPTER XIII

The winds were light the following day, as my life continued pleasantly on the island. Palm trees swayed, and coconuts flourished, as their milk flowed freely. Flora blossomed among the greens of the plant life, which took ecological dominance over the island.

Cindihan and I shared a tent, but a divider maintained our respective privacy. It was a comfortable place, and it became more so, as we got closer onward...

... she came to my side for a cuddle.

'Ah, my sweet,' I crooned at her, kissing her softly on the head.

'Your training should serve you well today in competition.'

'The Ordeal?'

She nodded...

... and I had to agree. 'Yes, I guess the bother shall be worth it.'

I sighed and wondered about the expectations placed upon participants. I've never done anything of this sort; to compete in crazy Olympic-styled events was not really my style...

... for I was a sailor, worth his trade.

I also wondered about Timbala, and how he was probably preening himself to such ends. *How did he fit in all this?*

I posed the matter to Cindy. 'Does the Chief engage as well?'

'Everyone does. Though there is a specific event which makes it possible to determine a new leader. Timbala had won this over many years, which is why most people just let him be, and not bother to topple him over.'

'Over what?'

'The edge, you silly!'

This should be good...

... this I've got to see.

'Tell me no further, I want to be surprised. The look on Hathaway's face should be priceless.'

'Who knows, maybe you or he will win.'

'Not taking sides, then?'

'No,' she grinned.

I waved the notion aside. 'Well, if I win, I couldn't do it. I'm no leader.'

'You could be,' she said, walking back to her side to get dressed behind her rude screen of division.

I got up and went to relieve myself in the brush outside. After re-wrapping the cloth around my waist, Timbala turned up.

'Hathaway,' I sneered.

'Now, now, Daye. That is between you and me. Respect, please.'

'You fool-button Englishman, I heard you can be dethroned.'

'Not in a million years, silver or not. You'll never get me, though the challenge will prove most infatuating.'

I smiled at him. 'Are you ready for it?'

He smiled back. 'Are you?'

His relief was assured...

... then he commented, 'After many years though, I am thinking someone is out there, wanting...'

'Cindihan's betting on me,' I boasted.

'Oh *is* she?' Timbala turned, his cape whirled around him, 'If you find yourself superior to me, then go out and show it.'

He adjusted himself and walked off; I smarted in the brush, feeling rather limited...

... but I would not let *him* get to me.

I returned to the tent and threw on a tunic and newer under cloth, a skimpy best which should reflect the challenge that lay ahead of me. Cindihan wore a longer tunic and tied her long honey-coloured hair back. We ate breakfast made up of fruits, nuts, bits of meat, and bread at the communal table. There were some wine and water caskets used, as well as freshly prepared coconut milk.

I reckoned these people had to be well prepared for what was to come.

After an hour of ceremonial prayers of thanks and hope to the gods, the Maltawah began the arm wrestling tournaments. Mostly men took part, but some women, who were eager to show off their skills, did likewise.

When it was my turn, I was paired with Ansarah...

... who would loom large in this year's Ordeal.

We clasped hands, pushing ourselves to the limit. His hand was very strong, led on by a muscular arm. Compared to my mere naval experience, he was something else...

... yet, I proved to be a formidable opponent to him.

He started sweating a little, as he tried to bring my hand down toward the table. I counter-balanced him and moved his to my side...

... soon, my hand reached the table and I'd won the round.

Ansarah shook my hand; then, Timbala awaited me.

I gasped, 'You?'

'I told you I'd be here. This is merely a warm-up. I must continue to prove myself to my people.'

'Excuse me, but it's *my* people,' I dared to correct him.

'Ah yes, your *better* half. Just remember, I'm still the Leader, so whachit,' he joked intentionally.

I disregarded the comment, and sat down with him to carry the next round. Our hands clasped, as we wrestled our way toward supremacy of the match. I held my ground, but Timbala stood firm too. He had become just as fit as the rest of the Maltawah, from being so many years on this island...

... and, in his opinion, better, due to his English ingenuity...

... but not as dark.

Smoke that in your primitive salons, Hathaway!

Soon, his hand quickly bounced to his side of the table.

'Gotcha,' he grinned triumphantly, 'I won this time.'

'All's fair that is fair,' I shook his hand...

... I got to stop my daydreaming, shit!

'Indeed, you are adapting to our ways. Most impressive,' he complimented.

'Not unlike yourself.'

'Wait and see.'

He walked off. *He should walk off a pier*, but I remained silent.

There were more engagements underway, which many Maltawah showing their definitions of stamina, endurance and determination. Stick fighting served these tests of skill, upon a long plank above a stream...

... and the winner was appointed, as soon as the opponent fell over into the water below.

Several members had turns and their stamina was assessed therein...

... and then I was up against Timbala...

... *again.*

Timbala and I used our long sticks, as if they were swords, but with both hands. Everyone was gathered to watch us from both sides of the stream. I took off my tunic, as the sun got stronger during the day; I also felt if I lost, the less clothes worn, the better.

I gave the tunic to Cindihan to hold and embraced her. 'Wish and hope for me.'

'No problem,' she whispered.

'Watch out, Daye, I may get the better of you yet and have Cindihan, too,' Timbala warned, less adorned than usual...

... *I figured jewellery and water didn't mix.*

'You've won above me, but here it goes,' I answered him with a blow that he actively blocked.

The struggle commenced and we beat against each other's sticks, trying to balance ourselves on the plank bridge.

I stared at him hungrily in the eye; he returned his vicious gaze back at me...

... blow after blow was had, with nothing too elaborate to overplay one's hand.

I asked the Chief, 'This is not the dethroning bit, is it?'

He laughed vigorously. 'No, and it will do you good to keep up with me.'

With that comment, he struck again, which I deflected. My instincts for action got the better of me, and I watched my counterpart trying to cleverly eye me in an off-direction, in order to get me...

... but this time, I took advantage of his own distraction...

... and prodded him off the plank, into the water.

Now, I got you, Timbala!

His pride sank many feet deep, yet he rose above the stream, unhinged.

'Daye, that was the most devious, devilish exercise of skill I have ever encountered. You do play fair and I like that. I shall enjoy further engagement with you, for the term is not over.'

'I deeply look forward to the pleasure, Silas Timothy,' I murmured.

He made a face at me, while climbing out and prepared himself for the next bit, as did I...

...for there were more ways to tip him off his pedestal.

In another section of the island, a huge, thick pole was erected a few feet high in the deeper part of the surrounding water. It was ironically proverbial, as it was a similar pedestal I kept referring to in my mind...

... however, this one was real and he was going to sit on it.

A rope ladder was extended from the top for climbing purposes. Timbala climbed first, unhindered, so he could get to his seat. A mechanism was rigged so when someone pressed a button at the top, but below the dais, the chair would tip backwards, releasing the sitter into the water. This also freed the climbing ladder, and everyone remaining got wet, too. The one who succeeds in 'dethroning' the sitter becomes the new leader.

It sounded fair and democratic; I found it much more *interesting* than the mere voting process of civilisation.

Once Timbala was seated, the climbers began their ascent. Moments of minor harassment overcame a few, as those below tickled those above them, and they lost their hold and fell into the water. This exemplified solid endurance, for if one touched another, it was only a matter of time, before...

... splash!

Then, those people were done for the day and newcomers had a go. Everyone loved to participate in this, Timbala especially...

... because he had a button beside him, and if he wished, he could release the rope and cast all his opponents into the stream...

... to retain his leadership status...

... which is what he did for many years, to secure his hold.

Naturally, over his tenure as Leader, many tribesmen and women wanted desperately to take him down, but he got them first...

... or they got each other.

More and more joined in to climb this sacred ladder of fortune, watching the lesser ones fall, and new ones ascend...

... making it more fun.

Little by little, inch by inch, the endless competitors strove to topple Timbala off, once and for all. He watched carefully, while the many climbers fell and climbed and fell again.

It wasn't long before Cindihan and I had a chance at the ladder, so we joined in...

... a chance to tumble the leader.

As I climbed, I reached up and lightly touched soft flesh, which soon surrendered to my being, as that person was tagged into a watery defeat...

... I carried on climbing...

... enjoying every succulent move toward the great Timbala...

... *ha-ha-ha.*

But when I got halfway, a lucky one got me in my spare parts, and I lost my hold on the situation...

... and in I fell...

...*sploosh!*

I bobbed up from the water, and cleared my face, when I saw my dear Cindihan waving at me and giggling...

... I gave her a look...

... then to her surprise, a tribesman got *her* where it counted...

... and soon she splashed down beside me.

I asked her, 'Good feeling?'

She kissed me in response and tickled my already stimulated loins...

... it was surely a pleasant dream to be had...

... but to each his own; *we didn't win.*

'He'll get his,' she observed. 'Those men up there are determined.'

'I cannot wait to see the results.'

'He's not all that anyway. He's no one and everyone, and he meant all the world to me.'

I turned to her, 'He just looks the part, but cannot act.'

'He's done it for many years, I think he's perfected his technique.'

'We're all getting older, Cindy, Timbala is not immune to age, you know.'

I later secretly agreed with her... *he wasn't all that.*

We went to the bank of the stream and scrambled onto the grass. We didn't think there was much money there anyway, nor were the Silver Millions present. We had a think and a giggle about this, while resting on the sweet land. It was nice to have a turn; better to have gotten it over with, and fun to watch others experience the same fate we had.

... though seeing Timbala himself fall would be a much better option.

He sat nervously, but watchful, as more and more Maltawah made their purposeful climb, in the hope of his dethronement.

He was tempted to press his button, fingering gently at a tease to release the ladder, preventing those climbers from reaching him. He goaded those opponents, eyeballing them with playful humour, despite the seriousness of the situation...

... for *any* tribesman might succeed in giving him a good bath, ascending into leadership themselves...

... whomever this may be.

Timbala remained lightly dressed in his dignity, only to cover up modesty. He sat there, showing that *he* was still the Leader...

... for the moment.

But as luck turned into outrageous fortune, someone was truly out to get him. Breathes exhaled at an alarming rate, the climbers became wetter in their mystique and desire to begin anew...

... and one man persevered...

... *Ansarah.*

He stealthily climbed through, bypassing the others, as they fell away to make room for him. He pursued that button which will release Timbala from his lofty place. Timbala had a good view, but every move he monitored, and continued his light fingering of the trigger, *ever so gently...*

... knowing if he failed, he would be forever deposed...

... not necessarily killed, though.

Cindihan and I waited and watched with those already tagged-out, and relieved they did their bit...

... *but this was agonisingly tantalising to watch.*

Both men met eye to eye, and soon, it became most clear. Ansarah felt, at last, he had a good chance to win. New climbers made their ascent and tried to topple over Ansarah, so they could have a go at the Chief. Ansarah stood his ground, desensitised himself from the endless feather-like touching around his person, and about to press the button...

... *when...*

... *at this point, Timbala knew the game was up.*

Oh God, my time had come. Uh-oh, I'm going down, Timbala shrieked to himself, as his delicious, hairy-chested pride dropped…

… he fell backward into the water...

... making him a *mortal like us* again.

The rope ladder was also discharged and everyone fell in after him, as ambition turned to a soaking defeat for the others...

... as it was Ansarah that did the honour of deposing Timbala...

... thus, making him the *new* Leader of the Maltawah.

Timbala ascended from the water, like the burning phoenix that he was, and went to Ansarah.

'Congratulations, you'd done it. I wondered when you would eventually get me,' he said, shaking Ansarah's hand.

'Your reflexes are not as quick as they used to be, eh,' was the quick answer.

'Maybe it was about time I backed down a bit. It was fun while it lasted, though,' Timbala admitted.

'Your self-defence over the years was most honourable.'

The former Chief nodded, and bowed his head toward Ansarah, 'I now concede to you.'

Ansarah also paid respect and did likewise. 'We will have a feast to celebrate my victory and instalment as the new Leader.'

I soon joined Timbala. 'Tough luck, huh?'

He grinned. 'Not at all. It was only a matter of time.'

Cindihan chimed in, 'I enjoyed your falling.'

'I am sure you did, my lovely girl,' then Timbala whispered to me, 'Actually, I wanted Ansarah to win. He has proven himself over much time to be the best of this lot. If this were an election, my vote would have been on Ansarah.'

I was surprised at this. 'You *wanted* him to win?'

'Shhhh, of course. Ansarah is a true-blood Maltawah. So, he fits in better than I. But don't tell him though. He may swell with too much pride, and that is a value I do not condone. Let him have his victory, while I sail away for England again.'

'You're going back?'

Timbala turned to me. 'I want to. As much as I loved it here, I really miss the civilisation I had been accustomed to in my younger days.'

'It'd changed since then,' I warned.

'Nonsense. People are people, whose nature never changes. Some have died, some are newly born, but the nature of things are the same. We are all greedy sods in th'end.'

He had a point. 'I was thinking of taking Cindihan back to Ireland with me, maybe marry her.'

'We had agreed that we would fight for her. Technically, you've won, but now it's her choice, my friend; I surrendered my status. However, if you do wish it so, may I be your best man?'

'Could do, yeah, Timbala,' I replied.

'You may call me Hathaway, Tim or Silas, if you please. Timbala has no further attribution for me now. It is only the Maltawah word for Leader.'

I cackled loudly, 'Would Silage do?'

Hathaway grabbed me and tossed me into the stream, laughing cruelly as I fell in. 'Nice to see the shoe is on the other foot now, eh??? Get dipped, Conna Daye!'

I popped my head up, spitting out water, and desiring to make a rude gesture, but refrained, due to the other Maltawah around us. I climbed out of the water and dried off.

And with that, we prepared for the evening's feast and Ansarah's induction as the new Timbala.

CHAPTER XIV

It was the day of Ansarah's installation as Timbala, Leader of the Maltawah. The tribesmen, along with their women and children, gathered together, chanting in Native tongue, '*Chunga, chunga, chunga.*' It was a sacred word to describe hugeness in size, and Ansarah was certainly huge today...

... at least in the mind, that is.

His ego inflated to oversee its appeal to its new status, as he marched in a procession with the former Timbala, Silas Hathaway. Ansarah was dressed formally in high-class Maltawah gear, adorned with a shell necklace, a multicoloured feathered headdress, and a windswept tunic, not unlike those once worn by Hathaway.

The procession approached a more stable throne, which stood firm in its glory, eager for a butt to sit on it. They stopped at the seat. Hathaway turned to Ansarah and chanted a few Native words, then he handed him his more sophisticated headdress of Leadership.

'You may need to adjust the band, for a more firmer fitting,' Hathaway advised.

Ansarah accepted the item; while taking off his own, he commented, 'I hope the bandwidth is not too wide for me. I will not be able to receive communication, thus. I would be honoured, though, if you do the adjusting, but it may take much to do so.'

Hathaway blushed at the quip, but laughed nonetheless. He took the headdress from Ansarah and placed it upon his head, and it fit... first time.

'I can see that my former crown is of an appropriate size. May you wear it well, and lead wisely by it, Timbala.'

Hathaway bowed to Ansarah, who replied, 'I do and I shall.'

More prayers were said and ceremonies fulfilled. Soon, all was concluded and the meal came thereafter. A relieved Hathaway strode up to sit beside Cindihan and me.

'Phew,' he exhaled, 'Glad that shit's over. I was right to yield the Title to him.'

'What makes you think Ansarah could do better? You've led the tribe for nearly twenty or so years,' Cindihan remarked.

'Ah, my dear Cindy,' Hathaway assured, 'You keep faith in Ansarah. He's the best. You were not here for as long as I, and not privy to witness the whole of my ruling here. I feel he'll do as well as me. He knows his people.'

I gobbled up my food, and in between bites of hot meat, I asked, 'So when are we leaving, then?'

'I'll have to arrange it with Ansarah. There are some derelict vessels on another part of the island that were kept on as souvenirs, for possible future use. Maybe he could get his men to rig one up for us. It is about time we went home. I'm itching to return.'

Cindy enquired, 'Where in England do you live?'

'I'm not sure. I was born at Sydmouth Harbour. From there, with so many ships, men, women bustling about... I am hazy about those years. You know how it is. Do forgive me,' Hathaway said.

'That's fine. I try to forget my crap, too.'

Hathaway smiled at her and gave her a kiss.

'Sydmouth Harbour,' I mulled aloud to myself.

Hathaway responded, 'Pardon?'

'Isn't that near a place called Totteringstate? You know, that pig farm that sells meats and soap products at the local market,' I recalled.

'I believe so, yes,' he confirmed. 'But how do you know about the estate?'

'We sailors get by,' I smiled, 'There's this Captain I'd served under...'

Hathaway chimed in quickly. 'That wouldn't be Captain Spey?'

'Yep, that's him. He is related to the Woodes-Hastings family, who owns Totteringstate.'

'Small world, eh,' Hathaway grinned.

'Only to grow bigger with exploration,' I firmly believed.

'And swollen with our people living in it, yours and mine,' he replied.

I chuckled aloud...

... the great British Empire, along with the hard working Irish, ready to conquer the world...

... I liked the sound of that...

... but there will be many others, too, with the same dreams.

'Instead of England, why don't we go further, like to the colonies, for instance,' I wondered.

'No… ah,' Hathaway shook his head. 'I wish to be reacquainted with the land of my birth, and reunite with my older brother. Maybe some other time.'

I asked, 'What's his name?'

'Noah James ' he replied.

He smirked to himself, while we still ate and drink to our heart's content. Ansarah sat at the head of the table, taller than most, in his fanciful position, eyeing all around his table. He was proud to be the Timbala, subtle as he was...

... and good looking too...

... as he would need to take on a wife, and there were many to pick from...

... *but that's another story.*

A booming voice called out, 'Hathaway!'

It was Ansarah. 'What are your future plans, now that you are no longer our Leader?'

'You know, I was hoping I can use one of those vessels beached at the other side of the island. We could make one seaworthy,' Hathaway answered.

'We will work together to do so,' Ansarah promised.

'Ah, good, I'd hate to swim all the way.'

'Don't push our generosity,' he warned.

'I plan to take Conna Daye and Cindihan with me.'

'That is fine. You three belong together somehow.'

I nudged at Hathaway to hush-it. He was alone in his mirth, but remained silent for the rest of the meal.

When the feasting was over, it was only a matter of time before we finally departed Profesthermeth Island.

A custom-made vessel was refurbished; salvaged from the others, it had men working on the damn thing night and day. Hathaway and I helped them; with our nautical knowledge, it made the task easier. It was large, able to fit the three of us. It had a body like Neptune and sails specifically designed to take on gusts of wind that will make them tremor.

We didn't pack much... *we didn't have much.* Some clothing that we used on the island we took with us, though food was the bigger priority. Hathaway had some bits of clothing from his old days, some of which fit me too. Cindihan had a few bits from her wrecked trip, which she packed away for this voyage.

Overall, we had a fair chance, and our goal (for now) was to make it to Europe, at least. I wondered if Ansarah was kindly, or *was he really trying to drive us away?* Hathaway may have yearned for the old country, as I did for mine, but I sensed a Native enthusiasm about the decree.

On the day we parted from the island, the wind was gentle and the water, most willing. The sky was a perfect blue and showed no hint of any craziness to come.

I asked Hathaway, 'Shall we sail forth?'

'Indeed,' he answered.

The three of us headed to the ship, which we christened *Timbala*, as a memorial to Hathaway's former role in life, and out of respect for the Maltawah.

'May the gods go with you,' Ansarah chanted, 'May you find your home soon.'

'I thank you, Timbala,' Hathaway responded with a bow, noting the new connection.

Cindihan and I also bowed before Ansarah and the Maltawah. I admitted to myself that the island would be sorely missed, and it had been a very pleasant stay here...

... especially now that I'd found my dream girl Cindy, though I still had reservations, regarding her relationship with Hathaway...

... I would have to test her on this sometime, if need be.

We boarded the *Timbala* to begin a new voyage. We raised anchor and sailed away. It was slow moving at first, yet the breeze moved us along toward open waters...

... and into a wavy sea.

CHAPTER XV

As we sailed along the cool and crisp water surrounding Profesthermeth Island, I found Cindihan helping Hathaway with the steering. He must have instructed her, while I was sorting the anchor into place. She made a good crewmate, and willing to learn the sailor's trade. I taught her further, on the ways and means of seamanship. She found it fascinating and found ways to implement her knowledge in our journey home.

After an hour or so into the wider ocean, the waves became stronger, yet we persisted, as faithful sons of the sea. Hathaway continued to steer, as I rummaged for maps within the cabins below deck. Then Cindy took over the helm, steady as she went, while Hathaway and I scoured through those maps to find civilisation.

We planned our trip...

... but what we hadn't planned for was the weather...

... which got rough in the next few days.

My senses revealed a sudden storm approaching and we tried to prepare for it. Then heavy, bitter winds started to play havoc with the sails, and the waves rocked our ship back and forth. I helped Hathaway with the steering, as I had Cindihan remain below deck, out of the way. It was a spartan crew, and I doubted we'd survive *this* ordeal.

I wanted to get below to check on Cindy. She jumped atop, and held me.

She cried out in a panic, 'What do we do?'

'Just hold on, we'll be fine,' I answered half-heartedly.

I dared not tell her the obvious.

Hathaway had other ideas. 'Return her below, Daye. This is too rough for a lady.'

'Too rough for us, too, I fear,' I replied back.

'You have no choice. Get her down, and help me with this.'

I grabbed her and carried her below. 'Hey,' Cindy shouted, 'What gives?'

'Captain's orders. This is too bad for you. Silas wants you out of the way.'

I flopped her back on the cabin bed and closed the door.

I returned atop to face the storm, like the man I was. So, along with Hathaway, we fought like devils to maintain the integrity of the ship during this bombardment.

However, if your nautical skill was too far stretched, prayer might be an option...

... to which I partook, whole-heartedly...

... and I prayed to anyone who'd listen...

... while keeping ourselves afloat, and in control of our meagre vessel.

And somehow, somewhere, the answer was found.

In the midst of the nasty foam around us, something scary emerged from the depths...

... scary to most, familiar to me...

... it was Chayten.

I called out to him at the top of my lungs.

Hathaway took one look at the beast and cowered beside me. 'What the fuck is that thing???!!!'

'Don't worry, Silas. I know him,' I assured.

He screamed, 'You *KNOW* him?'

Chayten smirked at our argument, and spoke his way with a keen growl. 'Having trouble with your ship?'

I snapped back, 'DUH! What do you think?'

'Well, I think you could use some help, but you will have to abandon her.'

Our ship... our measly stuff... we could buy more later... oh Christ, what the hell. 'I'll go get Cindy; I'll not leave her.'

I ran below to fetch the ol' girl.

'Cindy? Who's Cindy? I'm talking about the ship, you mortal dimwit,' the creature snarled.

Hathaway gave me a friendly slap on the head, as I passed. 'Dullard.'

'You'll have to climb on my back,' Chayten offered. 'Can ye do that?'

I soon returned with the girl, and put her upon the monster's back, with us following.

Chayten was amused. 'Got yourself a girlfriend, Daye?'

'Ha-ha,' I scoffed.

'And your twin, I see,' he continued. 'All family?'

'Shut up, he's not my twin,' Hathaway grumbled, 'But we are related.'

'Figures. You three look the part.'

In no less than minutes since mounting Chayten, the *Timbala* was sadly (but inevitably) demolished by the hungry, violent waves of the sea...

... it was an end to a different part of life...

... and this ending was felt by all of us...

... now, it was just us versus nature.

Chayten pulled himself up further. 'Ready?'

Hathaway snidely remarked, 'We've no choice, have we?'

'You don't,' I answered him with finality.

The monster announced, 'Let's go.'

Chayten then spread his wings out, liberating the silvery shimmer around him. They boosted him out of the water and into the more calmer skies...

... the storm had subsided by now...

... and we needed to push on...

(... *though not intending to do so on the back of a beast.*)

Riding through the sky was not for the faint-hearted.. As we hung on, I noticed the familiar scaling...

... the coins...

... or what you could make out to *look* like coins.

Now I realised why everyone on the *Taylor Brent*, as well as I, saw the Silver Millions. The intricate reptilian scaling looked deceptively like the amassed fortune. Naturally it was known about, but to see it up-close like this was a privilege not to be missed.

'Oh, and by the way, I've realised I'm from the future,' Chayten revealed, after many solitary days of wondering. 'I thought you should know. Your faces staring at my unique scaling tells it all.'

I already knew this, but Hathaway was astonished at his remark. Yet, we did not care. *We just wanted to get out of this alive.*

'Just get us the hell back to England,' Hathaway wailed, out of his fear of the creature and a slight height disorder.

'England, you say,' the creature confirmed, 'I will have to find a vessel to take you there. It has a flag at the front with two intertwining crosses, I believe.'

'Yes, Chayten,' I answered, 'You are right. It is the Union Jack. I'll keep a look out.'

'Why can't you take us all the way,' Hathaway moaned.

'It will take longer, if I did that, and I do not think the people of your homeland would delight in seeing a flying circus about.'

'Yeah, you ought to be put in one,' he retorted.

'Can it will, ya? He's my friend, and he's saving our lives, you ungrateful person,' I shot back.

Chayten paid no heed to Hathaway and carried on. Creatures were like that: dumb, forgiving and mostly meant to move on with things...

... if only *we* could.

A few miles past outwards, and only Heaven knew where we were (cos we didn't), a ship was sailing...

... and I recognised it immediately.

'That's my ship, the *Taylor Brent*,' I announced.

Cindihan glanced downward. 'Where?'

'Right there,' I pointed, quickly then grabbed a scale.

'OUWCH,' Chayten roared.

'Sorry.' I gave him an apologetic pat.

Hathaway was stunned. 'You're *that* friendly with this thing?'

'Common courtesy, you know,' I smiled back.

He shrugged his head, still holding on for dear life…

… as were we all.

'I guess this is where we part company,' the sea beast decided.

'It was kind of you to help us.' I gave him more reassuring pats.

'Jeez, he's going after the creature. Now, I've seen everything,' Hathaway muttered to himself. 'The gods were most fruitful today.'

I looked at Silas. 'Are you still a Maltawah or English, really?'

He laughed, 'Guess the Native ways hadn't left me.'

Chayten lowered himself closer to the water and shook us off his body, like a dog with wet fur. The three of us plunged into the sea and swam for the now nearby *Taylor Brent*.

CHAPTER XVI

As we got closer, the ship's hulking sides looked wildly familiar to me. I took Cindihan and quickly paddled with her, while Hathaway swam breast strokes on his own...

... and I still wasn't sure about him.

I called out and noticed some activity on deck. A tall man, wearing an open white shirt, and belted breeches, with a spyglass appeared. His hair was short and waving about in the light winds.   He spotted us, and rechecked his device to be certain. I got Cindy to wave at him to show we needed help.

'I'll cast a line out to you,' the man called out with cupped hands...

... it was dear ol' Captain Spey.

I swam toward Hathaway. 'Come closer, Spey's towing us in.'

'About time,' he remarked, pausing. 'Spey, you said?'

'The one and only.'

'The captain you referred to earlier?'

'Just grab the line and accept the offer, or I'll see that you drown.'

Hathaway relented his mutinous spirit, and towed the line along with us...

... but his grumbling continued. 'I can smell the arrogance a distance away.'

I gave Silas a not-so-friendly slap on the head. 'He's my Captain.'

'Was your Captain,' he noted. 'You told me you were lost at sea, remember?'

'He's still my Captain,' I insisted.

'Please yourself. Your loyalty is worth noting.'

'I thought tribal leaders would demand loyalty.'

Hathaway turned to face me. 'Doesn't mean *I* have to be.'

Soon, we were hoisted aboard the *Taylor Brent*...

... the ship which started my crazy story thus far...

... and greeted by Spey himself.

'Well, well, well, if it isn't crewman Daye and Company. I thought I'd seen the last of you. It's been so many months.'

'It felt like an eternity. Sorry about leaving you,' I said, 'This is Cindihan and Silas Hathaway.'

We shook hands, though the Captain kissed Cindy's hand.

'Go down below to get some dry clothes. Then report for your duties,' Spey ordered.

'What? I'm not one of your beggar's crew,' Hathaway protested.

'This is not a cruise ship, if you don't mind! If you wish to sail in her, you must work aboard her,' Spey reprimanded. 'The more hands the better and the sooner we could return home.'

There was the rub that got Silas thinking...

'Fine, I'll do it,' he relented, yet again.

'We've been at sea for many years altogether, for months at a spell. All the days are the same,' Spey explained. 'I'm more than happy to be standing out here with a ship to defend our Nation and Empire. Yet, what for... The Spanish? The Silver Millions? For my bloody health?'

The Captain panted out of his rave when I interjected, 'Hathaway's not used to serving like we do, sir. He was once a proud tribal leader of the Maltawah for about twenty years.'

Spey looked at him. 'It shows, but every man must do his share, if we are to return to England.'

Cindihan felt left out. 'Can I sail your ship, mister?'

He turned to her. 'My dear girl... can ye handle a ship?'

'I've been part of a crew with Conna and Silas aboard the *Timbala*, but we got wrecked in a storm and this Chayten fellow saved us.'

Spey's enthusiasm sunk like a battleship. '*The* Chayten?'

'Yeah, he's got a back full of coins, but they're really scales. We had a good look at them, cos we had to hang on during the ride he gave us,' she added.

'So *that's* what I saw in the sky, just before you were spotted... I think that's where our failure lies,' Spey sadly intoned. 'But there will be no failure today. Go get cracking, now move!'

He sent us away to change and return to report for duty.

Later, Cindy and I got to work together on rigging... *again.* Hathaway worked with Spey to find a suitable course home.

'We were heading that way anyway, when we located you,' Spey said. 'So we brought you aboard.'

Hathaway was most pleased. 'Thank you again and I hope we've earned our salt.'

'I think the three of you are worth more than the salt you were given,' the Captain implied.

'Please forgive my earlier behaviour. I meant no harm... it's just I...'

'You were once a leader of a distant tribe. Daye told me, remember? It is hard not to get used to being lowered when once you were up high. How it is that you are no longer a tribal leader?'

'Long story,' Hathaway replied. 'A sort-of election was held and I lost.'

'What do you mean *sort-of* election? I did not think natives were at all democratic.'

'The Maltawah have been exposed to our ways, but they do it... *differently,* and sort out their business and elections in competition.'

'As in sporting events?'

Hathaway stared at Spey. 'You could say that. I've thus eaten the pie of humility.'

'I guess it gave you indigestion,' Spey observed.

'More than you can say so, sir.'

He left it there and continued his chart work.

* * * * *

Days and weeks passed, our routines entrenched into our system. We continued this hopeful fair-weather journey home...

... but for me, I was to go to the island next door...

... and secure my rites with Cindihan at Oconnalow...

... *if she was willing*.

I needn't have bothered to ask, though, because as we worked together, we grew closer. I was her personal C.O. and she reported to me...

... *but one day, it was to become more personal.*

'You know, Conna, I think we ought to get married. It's like you love me, and I love you lots, with us working together and all that. Yes, it's been some time, and though I am fond of Timbala, or Silas, I think we know each other reasonably well.

'But he had shown his colours on the mast, so now I see he's a bit cowardly, don't you? Yeah, we *should* get married. Could we do so here, or do we have to wait? Like, you know...'

I held Cindihan tight, as an anchor splashed down in my mind's ocean. 'Are you sure about this?'

I felt sceptical, but...

She put me on her pedestal that no one could fall from,
Not even from a press of a button.
How I slipped in, so easily,
After his delicious fall from grace.

'Yeah. Silas is with Spey at the moment, and personally, I think he's a jerk, anyway,' she concluded with finality.

So, I needn't have tested her after all...

... but I had to be forgiving.

'His mind's set on other things... he's hardly the settling-down type. He's still in shock from his downfall.'

'It wasn't really a downfall much. It seemed like a quick bit of fun, really,' she sniggered.

'No it wasn't. It may have been a bit of fun for us, but for Silas, it ended his career as a Maltawah. I've got half the bloodline still; he's just got his Englishness. He was merely *looked after*. Remember that.'

'I will, Conna.' She gave me a hug. 'He's not used to being with the poorer masses, is he?'

'No, and it probably will take many masses to build him up again.'

'Why, is he Catholic?'

'Doubt he's religious altogether,' I smirked. 'His god is his ego. I doubt the whole of England will fit such an ego of a man.'

'That's why I prefer to marry you Conna. We got close and I want to become closer to you, ego or not.'

I kissed her forehead. 'I've got no ego, girl. Never had one. If you want to marry, then so be it; we will do so.'

'Yay!' Cindy jumped up and down and gave me a hug.

A few crewmen grumbled about the girly shriek that ran through the ship. Captain Spey was duly alerted to the presence, and *oh boy, there he was before us...*

... and demanded, 'I thought I told you to get back to work!'

I flew in the face of his oppression (*not that it really was, mind*). 'I just asked Cindy to marry me.'

He smiled and extended his hand to me. 'Congratulations, Daye.'

'Thank you.'

'You know I cannot perform the ceremony aboard, as I do not have the spare time. You two will have to wait 'til we dock at Sydmouth Harbour.'

'How long do we have?'

'Oh, by the crow, a few weeks maybe... a month even.'

Cindy whined, 'Awh, can't we get there faster?'

'Do you have a solution? Do you have a motor that goes putt-putt in the night? No? Well, stop your moaning. If he's good to you now, he'll be better and more seasoned for you in due time.'

She continued to pout when Hathaway emerged from the lower deck. 'Did I miss something?'

'Conna and Cindy are getting married,' Spey said.

Hathaway was gutted, but knew this would be the best outcome.

He extended his hand. 'Best man still?'

I accepted. 'Yes, of course. I'll not let you get away.'

Excitement filled the air, when Cindihan blurted, 'Spey cannot marry us. We have to wait to port.'

I suddenly remembered something... my heritage... *my Irish half...*

... a knotted commitment, as intricate as Celtic design.

'We could do a handfasting ceremony to tide us over,' I suggested.

Hathaway quipped, 'What's that?'

'An ancient Celtic ritual that binds two people together for a year and a day. It's been practiced through the centuries, with long-ago origins. It's informal, but the intention is solid. The couple gets their hands tied up, and they speak their commitment to one another. A formal wedding could be done later.'

'This ship's got plenty of rope to tie you two up for perpetuity,' Spey laughed.

'And as an addition,' Hathaway insisted, 'We'd throw you both into the water; *see how you like it*. Stuff like that was done on the Island. The Maltawah are a dedicated bunch, but had a casual formality about them. It isn't the look, but one's intention that counts.'

Yeah, and I know what counts, baby!

CHAPTER XVII

A small ceremony of handfasting was then agreed upon. Captain Spey had the honour of binding us, if only for now...

... the formality could be done later.

A long strand of specially decorated rope was made for the occasion. It was tied to Cindihan and me...

... hopefully until eternity, or beyond.

The ship's crew all stood firm as witnesses to this long forgotten practice. It wasn't as if these events took place every day, you know...

... and it wasn't every day that a lady was aboard a ship, either.

I looked around me to pick out my old crewmates present, if any. *Crews come and go; they die or get a transfer.* That was the way of the seas of the time. I acknowledged Jarris and Cateliffe among the roped-in men. Hathaway stood by, in his role as my best man.

Spey cleared his throat and began: 'Although this is something I had heard of, never in my career at sea had this been done before. Many years have passed, possibly centuries, since this ceremony was last performed. Most of us, more than likely, will never marry; by deed, we become flighty fathers. We've all led lives away from those we loved. In this case, here are two persons willing to be joined together in union, preferably in matrimony. Though I am unable to perform a marital union for them, I shall not refuse them. With this ancient rite of handfasting, a union can be engaged, if only to tide them over, until we reach port.'

A pause was held for reflection…

… as Spey continued, 'Seaman Conna Timalyn Daye, do you wish to be informally bound to Cindihan, until such time approaches when you may finalise or terminate this union?'

I stared out toward Cindy, *knowing I'll be doing this again*, I claimed the magic words, 'I do.'

'Cindihan, do you wish to be informally bound to Seaman Daye, until such time approaches when *you* may finalise or terminate this union?'

She responded immediately. 'I do.'

'Then, with the rope symbolising your commitment to one another, I declare you both bound. When we reach Sydmouth, I strongly recommend you seek finalisation. Congratulations.'

I kissed Cindy and we embraced. Everyone clapped their support for us, when suddenly two crew members lifted us into the air.

To explain this, Hathaway contributed his tuppence. 'As we are still at sea, I thought to include a little something more personal, as a result of my defeat at Profesthermeth Island.'

As we were hoisted, he called out, 'Throw them in.'

We were both thrown overboard, tied and bound to one another.

Spey was shocked, and took Hathaway aside. 'What the blazes was that all about?'

'You stated this was informal,' he explained, 'Well, I mentioned earlier that I'd give the couple a well-washed send-off.'

'What *has* happened to you on that island, Silas?'

'Never mind,' he grinned, 'Let's fish the crazed couple out.'

In the water, I desperately tried to unbind myself from the rope, to allow myself and Cindihan to paddle and keep afloat. I quickly loosened the rope and cast it aside. Cindy grabbed me to hold on and regain some control in the wild wet sea. Another rope was lowered to us, and we used it to climb back aboard.

Hathaway greeted me. 'So sorry, Conna. This had to be done. You cannot be unbound now. You're in it for good.'

'You lost Cindy, that's all,' I uttered.

'I haven't lost everything,' he replied optimistically. 'I have a plan for when we return.'

'Oh?'

He flashed a wicked smile. 'You'll see.'

I thought nothing of his reaction and just spent the rest of the time with Cindihan. My duties were suspended for awhile, gladly filled in by other crew members, as a parting gift from Spey.

* * * * * *

The rest of the journey to England ebbed and flowed. It wasn't all smooth sailing, but with the addition of Hathaway to our usual bunch, it made for easier work.

Cindy spent time reading and helping me with light duty on the rigging. Her time in the mess was most fruitful, as she helped dish out solid hearty meals for us. I held back from her, though, despite our new union. I wanted to make meaning with her when we reached Oconnalow. She fit in well with the ship's crew, so she wasn't the biggest tease on toast. I got by with simple kissing and fumbling about.

I looked forward to disembarking and though to marry her at *St Elmo's-at-Sea*, a mariner's chapel built for the quick convenience of most sailors and their respective partners. Most of these unions were desperate, and when a newborn was involved, the matter got complicated. Thankfully, we took our love in stride and stayed careful between us...

... for there were other ways to love a woman...

... and I wanted to save *that* part of myself for last.

Several weeks went by and the voyage home took its toll on us. It wiped us clean of any emotion and we were all tired and needed a good rest on land. My love for Cindihan was sorely tested, and I found Spey's earlier comment to be prophetic. We lived hand-in-pocket together, as well as dealing with the others on the ship. Spey's discipline was fair, but not bordering on harsh extremity; we all knew our boundaries...

... and knew not to expand beyond them.

As we got closer to our destination, the inevitable *'Land Ho!'* was shouted loudly, as we scrambled to prepare ourselves for docking. Spey took out his glass and scanned the area. The warm familiarity of Sydmouth Harbour could not be missed. We even shaved off a few days, thanks to Hathaway's sharp knowledge of the seas. The trip took us around the world, which seemed like forever.

The boys aboard were on their best behaviour and knew not to mess with the Captain. They went about their tasks, minimal or of due importance, inching closer to their fulfilment of reaching home...

... a cosy, loving place, even if it was a barstool in a local tavern...

... it still qualified as home.

For me, home lay a bit further afield, but not as far gone. I consented to remain in England for a time, so further transport to Ireland could be arranged for me and Cindihan. I also decided to marry her harbour side, and touch Irish soil as a fully married couple.

Hathaway came up to me. 'Remember I told you I had something in mind?'

'Yes,' I recalled. 'Do tell, please.'

'Well, when we dock, my brother Noah James will meet with us, and I've made a decision.'

I was intrigued. 'Oh?'

'I want to sail for the colonies and bring Noah with me. Maybe you and Cindihan can join us, if you're interested.'

I shook my head. 'I love the offer, Silas, but I want to return to Ireland, settle in with Cindy, have a family, and walk on solid ground, thank you.'

It looked like I put a damper on his tremor of thought...

... but he wasn't phased. 'Suit yourself. I just wanted you to know.'

'You told me you wanted to stay in England.'

'Yeah, well, I changed my mind.'

'Up for more adventure, are you?'

Silas smiled. 'I am.'

'I had enough to last me a lifetime.'

'You just want to secure those rites at Oconnalow,' he laughed.

'That's right, I do. It means much to us Dayes,' I defended.

'What about after? Do the rites tell you to remain in Ireland, or move onto greener pastures?'

I folded my arms. 'Nothing is more greener than Ireland, matey. I've got a woman who needs to plant her roots somewhere, which are most fertile in Oconnalow.'

'I'll bet,' Silas grinned wildly, then thought about Cindy's crude beginning. 'I remember her roots being most shallow.'

'Yes, and I want to give her something she could be proud of.'

'You do that, Conna. You do that.'

I walked away from the conversation to find the crew preparing to land at Sydmouth.

CHAPTER XVIII

The harbour loomed larger as we nearly completed our journey. The weather stayed cloudy through the daylight; it gathered momentum toward our new destiny. I held Cindihan close. Hathaway filled in my working hours, so I could spend more time with her. Spey knew my heart wasn't all there anyway, so he continued the needed break.

I asked her, 'Looking forward to your new home?'

'Can't wait. I have not been here before. This is so exciting.'

'Cannot be any different from what you'd known.'

'Places are all alike,' she said, 'It is the people who make the difference. I can safely argue that in my case, *this is better*. Anything's better than *them*.'

I didn't like the trip down memory lane... *her* memory lane.

'Now hush up about that. They're gone and Silas, as Timbala, declared you normal like the rest of us. So, enough about that,' I persisted.

She sulked and sighed, knowing I was right in my exclamation. She looked pretty in her sand coloured tunic. I think a bit of shopping would do her some good. *She could use some more civilised gear...*

... as could I.

A few hours passed and Sydmouth Harbour was closer in the fair distance...

... and soon...

... thud!

The *Taylor Brent* finally made port and lowered its gang-plank. We officially departed onto dry land. It was good to feel cobblestone again, compared to the sandy terrain on the Island. Hathaway's brother, Noah James, was waiting in the crowd that clamoured to receive their loved ones and fellow drinking buddies. We followed him, as it was best we stick together.

Noah greeted us with charm and surprise. 'Discharged from the seas already?'

Silas replied, with equal charm. 'I wasn't really part of the crew. I was an add-on. Conna Daye is the true seaman here.'

I blushed, as we were introduced. 'Nothing official, really. I was declared lost and departed.'

'So you were declared dead, then,' Noah concluded.

'Being lost at sea is just as good as dead,' Silas explained. 'This little lady here found him washed up on my shoreline, after a haphazard spell as a Mercaste.'

Noah dismissed the mythology and noticed my wife. 'And this is...'

She extended her hand. 'Cindihan.'

'She's my informal wife,' I told Noah. 'We're planning to marry properly soon.'

The brother was puzzled. 'How so?'

'A handfasting ceremony was performed on the ship,' Silas clarified. 'Spey couldn't do a proper wedding for them, so what was done was an *informal bonding*.'

'*St Elmo's-At-Sea* should provide a goodly venue for you,' Noah offered.

Silas asked Noah, 'Where are you staying?'

'The *Horse & Dragon*. I can arrange some rooms for you. I'll make some enquiries.'

He and Silas went off to the inn and Captain Spey came up to us, while waiting for them.

'Didn't think I'd forget you, eh?' he said, 'So when's the big day?'

'Soon,' I assured him. 'Let us get settled first.'

'I see. You know, I will not expect you to return to ship.'

I looked at Cindihan, and lamented to Spey. 'True. I shall not. I wish to return to Ireland and start anew with Cindy. It was grand to work with you all, and your performance of the handfasting ritual was most appreciated. It gave us definition.'

I embraced her; Spey noticed this. 'No problem and I wish you all the luck of the world. It seems your people have got the monopoly on it.'

I sniggered at his comment.

'I'll stay docked until my next voyage to *Admiralty-Knows-Where*, across the seas. If you finalise your union before then, I would like to attend,' he continued.

'Silas's brother recommended the mariner's chapel, *St Elmo's*.'

'Good move. I'll be at the *Horse & Dragon*. Do contact me when you secure your ropes more firmly.'

'I intend to, sir. We're staying at the same place.'

'Very well. Don't be a stranger.'

Spey and I shook hands and he left, as Noah returned.

'The rooms are secure,' Silas spoke, 'I'm dying for a drink.'

'I think we all need one,' I agreed and off we went.

* * * * *

A couple of days later, Silas arranged a smart and simple dress for Cindihan, while I, too, attempted to look my best. I dressed without the frills of the fashion, but Cindihan looked beautiful in a cream coloured, full length gown. Silas and Noah attained their dress together, they being of similar size, despite the decade-old age difference.

We later headed for *St Elmo's-At-Sea* and had a simple service. Not many attended, except for a few members of the *Taylor Brent*, Captain Spey, and the two Hathaway brothers.

It wasn't customary for people off the streets to enjoy the spoils of a nuptial ceremony, but our wedding was news around town. Some of them were invited to stand as witnesses, and the more of them, the better.

I felt ecstatic on the day, while Cindihan looked like succulent sunshine on the beach. As it was a sunny day, the descriptive suited her (*as did the dress, when I eventually saw it*).

I explained to the priest beforehand about the handfasting ceremony we did on the ship. He understood and took it into account.

'You will have to properly verbalise your vows according to Church law,' he said...

... and I was more than happy to do so...

... in front of the whole congregation watching, as we waded through the multi-questioned brigade.

'Do you Conna Timalyn Daye, take Cindihan...'

'I do,' I affirmed.

'Do you Cindihan, take Conna Timalyn Daye to be...'

'I do,' she so stated.

'By the power vested in me, before this fair audience, I now pronounce you man and wife. May no man put asunder what the Lord has joined in holiness.'

Silas giggled and whispered something to his brother.

The rest went smoothly, then the pardons and congratulations were bestowed upon us.

In the wild evening, we had dinner with the brothers.

'I discussed my proposal with Noah and we've made a decision,' Silas began.

Noah's face went grim, but firm. 'We both decided to sail for the colonies.'

I had a feeling this was coming, from an earlier conversation I had with Silas. *It seemed it was intentional, thus, and his ego would surely fit there.* 'I shall miss you. I had a whale of a time with you, Silas.'

'And I with you,' he responded. 'But it is best we travel the broad sea and catch the distant highlights.'

I then asked, 'Is this why you really gave up your leadership of the Maltawah?'

Silas nodded, 'Yes, it was. You should have seen those green-envy eyes of the tribesmen. They hungered for the role so badly, and I'd hogged it up for so many years. I just felt it was time for me to just, go. I really want to move on, and find a girl of my own, like you did. Maybe in a generation or so, our descendants could become friends, uniting in a most unusual way.'

'That'll be the day,' Cindy tittered, 'The world's a big place, sir. That land of the Americas is even bigger, so they say.'

'Ah, but how much of it is occupied?' Silas challenged. 'And furthermore, I am no longer a *sir* to you. I am now your kinsman.'

Cindihan fell meekly silent, and went back to eating her pot-pie.

'Sorry, I forgot,' she bent her head down as she ate.

I pulled her up. 'Hey, you're family now; totally, unequivocally, and officially, Cindihan Daye.'

She smiled back at me, gracing me with a hug, exclaiming, 'Oh Conna! Oh Conna!'

I sighed. *Was this a re-enactment of how Oconnalow was created and so named?*

* * * * * *

A week later, we sailed home upon a packet bound for the colonies. These ships had a habit of picking up stragglers from port towns, along the edges of Britain and Ireland, before making the transatlantic crossing. Oconnalow was on the way, so I paid the tickets for me and Cindihan to depart for the Irish coast...

... while everyone else raced their hopes and dreams in the opposite direction.

Parting with the Hathaway brothers was crude and cruel on the outset. Despite his rough-tough jagged edges, and amorous advances to Cindihan in an earlier time, I enjoyed Silas's company. There was a comfort, too, in knowing that he was now truly *family*. Noah was a good counterpart, but far more formal and civilised...

... and it would be interesting to see how those two get on in a few decades' time in the colonies...

… but the loss now was already duly felt.

'My heart goes with you, Silas. May your voyage be steady and peaceful,' I said, hugging him.

He returned the hug. 'I wish you and Cindihan the best of everything. Someday we shall meet again; if not, in a few generations time.'

I laughed at the repetitive comment, not figuring on how *that* would be possible. I then shook Noah's hand, 'It was good to meet with you.'

Silas turned to Cindy. 'My dear, it was good to know such a unique person as yourself. I so wished it were me who'd won, and then maybe, I'd have you.'

'I am honoured to meet such distinction, too. Yet, it seems we have separate paths to travel,' she sighed.

He gave her a kiss. 'The moment I laid eyes on you, I knew you were special and better than the scum we deleted off the boat. I was right to give you a chance with the Maltawah, and I am glad to have respected you, intact.'

She smiled and kissed him back. 'Don't fall back overboard this time.'

Silas laughed at her comment, as his personality became lighter, yet sadder.

As the port of Queens-Cobhayr came into view, we traded hugs and handshakes for the final time.

My bones turned to jelly, just off the Irish coast, as I swelled with all the pride in my heart to be returning home. We disembarked there, and a west-bound crowd engulfed the space we once occupied. From nearby Cobh's Reach, I saw the ship continue in the fair distance, on its journey toward that Land of Hopeful Glory.

I unconsciously called aloud, 'Who knows what lay there?'

Cindihan overheard me. 'Pardon?'

'Forget it. My prayers go with them. Now, we make for Oconnalow.'

'Yes, let us forth into your primeval dwelling,' she aired proudly.

* * * * *

In the distant spell of time, I finally had my rites with Cindihan...

... just like Conna and Lowry did...

... all those centuries ago.

And what of the dear Hathaway brothers?

Word got out that the ship landed safely and docked at New York a few months later...

... give or take a week.

And how did I know?

A certain special sea creature told me so.